CANDY HARPER

SIMON AND SCHUSTER

First published in Great Britain in 2015 by Simon and Schuster UK Ltd
A CBS COMPANY

Copyright © 2015 Candida Harper

1 3 5 7 9 10 8 6 4 2

Simon & Schuster UK Ltd
1st Floor
222 Gray's Inn Road
London WC1X 8HB

Simon & Schuster Australia, Sydney
Simon & Schuster India, New Delhi

A CIP catalogue record for this book
is available from the British Library.

PB ISBN: 978-1-4711-2417-4
EBook ISBN: 978-1-4711-2418-1

Printed and bound by CPI Group (UK) Ltd, Croydon, CR0 4YY

www.simonandschuster.co.uk
www.simonandschuster.com.au

For my parents, who've got five
'little treasures' of their own

CHAPTER ❤ ONE

There's way too much talking about knickers in my house. I'm pretty sure that other people's families talk about pizza for tea and what they did at school. In my family, it seems like someone is talking about knickers every other day.

My biggest sister, Amelia, goes on about how her knickers are too babyish for a nearly-fourteen-year-old. My little sister, Lucy, likes to keep us updated about who in Year Two has wet their knickers, and my next sister up, Chloe, is always putting knickers on her head. Which I think is a little worrying for a twelve-year-old, but then Chloe will put anything on her head. Except shampoo.

Today's knicker chat started when everybody was supposed to be dressed and ready to go.

'I can't find any pants!' Lucy shouted.

Mum came out of the bathroom, brushing her teeth with one hand and putting on mascara with the other. 'There must be some somewhere,' she said, spraying toothpaste over Chloe who was sitting in the middle of the landing, eating a sausage. I don't know where she found the sausage. I only got cornflakes for breakfast.

Mum climbed over Chloe and went into the bedroom I share with Lucy and Chloe. She reached for the handle on Lucy's drawer.

'No!' Lucy shouted. 'Don't go in there! It's got secret things in!'

'I'm not trying to uncover your secrets. I just want to find you some knickers.' Mum swallowed her toothpaste. 'But Lucy, it had better not be the kind of secret that starts to smell funny after a few days.' She turned to me. 'Ella, you haven't got any of Lucy's knickers in your drawer, have you?'

I shook my head. 'None of Lucy's and none of mine. Chloe hasn't got any either.'

Chloe put the last of the sausage in her mouth. 'Can't we just wear yesterday's?' she asked.

'No!' Mum snapped. 'Honestly, I spend enough of my life doing the washing; how can all of your underwear suddenly disappear?'

'It goes to the same place that all the hairbrushes,

scissors and batteries do in this house,' Amelia said from her bedroom doorway.

She was looking so smug that I guessed she'd got a nice fresh pair of knickers on underneath her black jeans.

'Amelia, have you got clean pants? Could you spare a few pairs for your sisters?'

I don't know why Mum even bothered to ask. I can't remember the last time Amelia said yes to anything. Amelia looked at Mum with one cross eye. (The other one is hidden under her new fringe. I haven't seen it in months. Amelia's auburn hair is super smooth and shiny so she can make it sweep across one eye. I couldn't do that. My hair sticks up all over the place. And it's more what you would call carroty than auburn.)

'What happened to the system?' Mum asked us. 'I thought we agreed that when clean washing comes in from hanging on the line it goes in the basket under the stairs and then everyone is responsible for putting their own things away.'

'The basket isn't there any more,' I said.

'Lucy used it to bobsleigh down the stairs,' Amelia added.

Lucy stuck her tongue out at Amelia. 'I only did that after Chloe kept a hedgehog in it! A hedgehog is worse than bobsleighing.'

Mum sighed. 'Ella, go and look on the sofa. I think there was some clean washing abandoned there. If you'd all just put things away tidily, this wouldn't happen.'

'What's the point of putting things in drawers?' Chloe asked as I whizzed down the stairs. 'We'd just have to take them back out again. In fact, I don't even know why we bother taking things off in the first place.'

'So we don't end up smelling like you,' Amelia said, screwing up her nose.

On the sofa, I discovered two plates and Lucy's coat. Under the cushions were five pens, a satsuma (so old it had dried out and become more like a small brown rock), my missing homework and about a loaf's worth of crumbs. Finally, jammed between the sofa and the wall, I found a tangle of clean socks like a nest of snakes and five scrunched-up pairs of knickers. 'Found some!' I shouted and carried them back upstairs. There were three pairs of Mum's, one of mine and one of Chloe's. I grabbed the ones that belonged to me and threw Chloe's pair at her.

'Don't need them,' she said. 'I improvised and used my bikini bottoms.' She flashed me her behind; it was covered in shiny red fabric with little anchors on.

Seeing as we were running out of options, I offered Mum's knickers to Lucy.

'I can't wear them! They're big old lady pants. I'm seven. I need knickers that say seven on them.'

'At the moment, all the knickers for seven-year-olds seem to be under your bed,' Mum said, getting up off her hands and knees. 'We'll talk about why all the teaspoons are keeping them company later.'

'Why don't you put on your bikini bottoms like Chloe?' I suggested to Lucy.

'OK. Are we going swimming?'

'No, we're going to the hospital,' I said.

'Have they got a swimming pool?'

'No.'

'Then I'm not wearing my bikini.'

'We're going to miss visiting hours at this rate,' Mum said and she banged on the bathroom door, which Amelia had just locked behind her.

'I don't know why we're bothering,' Amelia's muffled voice said through the door. 'I've got enough crybaby, bare-bum sisters around here. I don't need to meet another one.'

Everyone went quiet.

Mum took a deep breath. 'Lucy, put your pyjama shorts on under your skirt. I'll buy everyone new knickers when I'm in town tomorrow and these ones had better be looked after.'

Lucy squealed. 'I want hearts on mine! No, kittens! No, racing cars! Kittens *in* racing cars!'

Amelia opened the bathroom door. 'I don't want anything frilly. In fact, don't buy me anything from the children's department at all.'

'Can you get me those ones with the flap at the back?' Chloe asked. 'Like in the olden days when they kept their underwear on all winter?'

My sisters all had loads to say about new knickers.

But nobody wanted to talk about my dad's new baby.

CHAPTER ✿ TWO

My nana always said that if your basket seems heavy you should remember that's because it's full of berries. That was kind of a joke because our surname is Strawberry. But basically it means try to ignore the bad stuff and look on the bright side. For example, I try to forget about how much people laugh when they see my red hair and hear my name is Strawberry; instead, I concentrate on being happy that I'm not my Year Six teacher. Her name is Mrs Bottomley.

When my parents first got divorced, everything was difficult. My mum was all quiet and sad, and Amelia was always telling us how horrible things were. I remembered what my nana said about berries and I tried my best to think about bright sides. It was hard, but it helped a little bit.

But now there is a definite bright side to my dad having a new girlfriend, Suvi, and that is that I've got a new sister. The bright side of sisters is that – even though sometimes they're annoying and put cream cheese in your bed – they are always your sister and that means they're always on your team. So it was weird that Dad had this new family, but now we had another sister and I was glad about that.

When we finally made it to the hospital, we all bundled out of the car, but Mum stopped outside the main entrance. Since my parents split up (one year, four months and sixteen days ago), there are lots of places that my mum doesn't come inside. Like Granny's house, and my dad's new house where he lives with Suvi, and the leisure centre where Dad takes us swimming. Instead, she just drops us outside. It seemed like the hospital was Dad's too.

'He should be here,' Mum said.

Amelia nodded. 'He's so unreliable.'

Chloe pulled a face at Amelia. 'Maybe Dad's waiting for us inside.'

Mum looked at her phone. 'He said he'd meet us here. Lucy, what are you doing?'

People always think Lucy is adorable because she's tiny and has reddy-gold curls, but if you watch her for two minutes you can see that, even though she looks like an angel, she isn't one. At this moment, she was scratching under her arm with one hand and had the other one stuck up her skirt.

'I can't help it,' she said. 'These shorts are making my bottom wiggle.'

'You look like you're trying not to pee,' Chloe said.

'You don't pee with your bottom! Your bottom is for p—'

'Your bottom will be kicked if you don't stop embarrassing me,' Amelia said. She pulled her black hat further down and held her book up over her face. I think she was pretending she wasn't with us.

'There he is,' Mum said.

I could see Dad through the big glass windows, making his way between people in the crowded reception area. He's really tall, like me, and his legs extend in these long, smooth strides that make him look like a dancer or an athlete when he walks. Not like me.

Mum pushed her bag up her arm. There was a long trail of tissue paper and the sleeve of a cardigan hanging out of it. 'Your dad said he'd drop you back at the house. I'll see you all later.'

'Aren't you coming in?' I asked. I knew she

wasn't, but sometimes you have to ask a lot of questions to get even a little bit of the real answer.

Mum shook her head.

Amelia scowled. 'Can't I come home with you?'

'No, your dad wants you all here. Anyway, I'm not going straight home. I've got some things to do.'

'I've got things to do!' Amelia snapped.

'Yeah, she needs to lie on the sofa, eating crisps and telling us how stupid we are,' Chloe said.

Chloe and Amelia always say rude things to each other. It used to make them both laugh, but now it just makes them cross. The rude things haven't changed, but maybe Amelia and Chloe have.

Amelia opened her mouth to say something mean back, but then Dad came out of the double doors. 'Hello, girls!'

Chloe threw herself on him.

'Louise,' Dad said, looking at Mum and ruffling Chloe's messy ginger hair. 'Thanks for bringing them.'

Mum smiled with her mouth, but not the rest of her. 'How's baby?'

'She's gorgeous. Looks just like Suvi.'

Mum's forced smile fell off her face.

'She's managed to avoid my nose anyway.'

'Wish I had,' Amelia muttered.

'So everything all right then?' Mum said, half turning to go.

'Yes, brilliant, marvellous.'

Mum nodded. 'Bye then, girls. Be good.'

I wanted to hug Dad, but Chloe still had her arms round him.

'Is the baby tiny?' I asked. 'Has she got a name yet? What colour is her hair?'

'Slow down! You can see for yourself in a minute. Amelia, are you coming or do you want to hang about in the car park looking moody all day?'

Amelia's eyes were fixed on Mum's disappearing back. 'You don't actually mean staying in the car park is an option, do you? Because if it is I'll definitely do that.'

Dad's lips twitched. I couldn't tell if it was a nearly-laugh or a nearly-shout, but it turned into A Look. When my dad gives me A Look, it makes me squirm like Lucy wearing pyjama shorts instead of knickers, but Amelia just shrugged and followed slowly. We walked into the hospital and over to a row of lifts.

Up on the fourth floor we found Suvi holding a very small baby with a fuzz of blonde hair. Nobody said anything.

'Wow,' Chloe said eventually. 'Is that a drip in your hand? Does it hurt when they stick it in? Josh

11

Williams in my class had to have a thing in his arm and they stuck it in the wrong place and he had a bruise the size of a cowpat an—'

'This is your new sister,' Dad interrupted, using the same voice as when he showed us our bedroom in his new house.

Nobody had liked that much either.

Amelia looked out of the window.

'She doesn't look like me,' Lucy said quietly. 'Her hair is the wrong colour.'

I felt sorry for the baby. She seemed like quite a nice baby and when she got a bit bigger I was sure she'd be brilliant. It wasn't her fault that we were cross with Dad.

'Ah,' I said. 'She's cute.' The problem with 'ahs' is that they have to just come out. If you do them on purpose, they sound stupid.

Amelia obviously thought so because she gave me her you-sound-stupid look.

'We've decided to call her Kirsti,' Suvi told us.

'Oh,' Lucy said. 'I thought you'd call her a crazy Finnish name, you know, like Suvi.'

'Kirsti is a Finnish name,' Suvi said.

'Are you sure?' Chloe asked. 'Because it sounds completely normal.'

'Can I hold Kirsti?' I asked.

'Yes,' Dad said.

'Maybe later,' Suvi said. 'She's just got to sleep. And it takes a long time to get her off. She's a fusser.'

'How do you know?' Amelia asked. 'You've just met her. You can't know anything about her.'

The rest of our visit was Dad oohing and aahing and taking photos to show us how great everything was, and Amelia's face telling us it wasn't.

Later that night, when I was in bed, I started thinking about Suvi and Kirsti and wondering what the others thought about Dad having a new family. To me it seemed like it had all happened very quickly.

Chloe and Amelia used to share a bedroom, but, after Mum and Dad split up, they kept falling out so Chloe moved in with me and Lucy. I sleep on the bottom of the bunk beds and Chloe sleeps on top. Lucy was already asleep on the other side of the room so I stretched up a leg in the direction of the top bunk and poked Chloe's mattress with my foot.

'What?' she whispered.

'Do you mind that Dad doesn't live here any more?' I whispered back.

'We didn't see him loads when he did live here. He was always at work.'

'But do you wish he still lived here?'

Because my dad has been gone for less than a year and a half, sometimes, when I wake up in the morning, I think for a moment that I can hear him in the bathroom or running down the stairs.

'He doesn't live here,' Chloe said. 'He's not going to move back, Ella.'

She didn't sound sad.

'Do you like Suvi?' I asked.

'She isn't exactly the one I would pick.'

'Who would you pick?'

She thought for a moment. 'An ice-cream van driver. A rich one. Who was really good at rugby.'

'I can't even imagine Suvi eating an ice cream.'

Suvi mostly seems to eat raw vegetables and things with seeds in.

Another thing my nana used to say was that when life gives you lemons you should make lemonade. That means doing the best with what you've got. But it's quite hard to think of a bright side to the person who your dad decided to love instead of your mum.

'She is quite tough,' Chloe said after a while.

'Suvi?'

'Yep. Most people cry when Amelia is mean to them; Suvi hardly notices.'

Chloe was right. Suvi doesn't seem to get

worked up about anything. Amelia says she's cold; she calls her the Ice Queen.

'And she's strong. She does all that yoga and she's got quite muscly arms. Basically, if we ever get attacked by aliens, I think she'd be a good person to have around.'

I sighed. Even though I know she's not trying, sometimes I think Chloe is better at looking on the bright side and making lemonade out of lemons than I am. When life gives her a frosty stepmum, she makes her into a soldier for her army against aliens.

CHAPTER ✦ THREE

'I got new knickers for everyone,' Mum said the next day at teatime. One end of the table was completely covered by a castle Lucy was making out of a cardboard box and Pringles tubes and yoghurt pots so we were all squished up at the other end. Mum was eating peas while tapping at her laptop which was wobbling about on her knees.

'Why are you allowed to have that at the table, but I can't have my phone?' Amelia asked.

'I'm working,' Mum said.

'You're always telling us not to leave things to the last minute,' Chloe said.

Mum still had tons of work to do before she went back to teaching Year Two next week.

'I know, but I didn't want to waste the holidays

on work when I could spend time with you girls instead.'

We had a brilliant summer. We stayed in a caravan in Cornwall, then we visited my cousins, and even when we were at home my mum thought up theme nights and competitions for us. She's really good at finding fun things for us to do.

Mum picked up a folder and a load of bits of paper fell on the floor. She isn't so brilliant at being organised.

'Did you get the rest of my new uniform?' I asked her.

'Uniform? Um, yes, it's on your bed,' Mum said. 'Except tights, but I'll get those really soon. I absolutely won't forget.' She wrote TIGHTS! on a Post-it note and stuck it to her laptop.

On Monday, I was starting Year Seven at St Mark's where Amelia and Chloe went. The bright side of going to secondary school was that my two best friends would finally get to meet each other. I didn't exactly have loads of friends, but I did have two brilliant ones and I wanted us all to be friends together more than anything. If you have friends then people don't laugh at you. Or, even if they do, you don't care so much because you've always got someone to be nice to you.

When I was little, we lived in London and I had

two best friends. It was fantastic: we did everything together and, even when one of them was ill, I still had someone to play with. But then we moved here. I think it's safest if you go to nursery and primary school and secondary school all in the same place; that way you always know someone. It's quite a stupid idea to arrive in the middle of Year Three when everybody has already got their own group of friends, but nobody listened to me when I said I didn't want to move.

Amelia and Chloe had no problems fitting into our new school. Chloe is so friendly and energetic that no one can help liking her and Amelia is so smart and funny that people feel lucky to be her friend. I don't really stand out like they do. I never know what to say to people when I meet them. For the first two weeks at our new school, I hid in the bushes at playtime. Then one day this girl called Kayleigh tapped me on the shoulder. She had brown, shiny hair like a conker, which was falling out of a ponytail. She smiled at me and said, 'Let's play unicorns.' So we did. Everybody liked Kayleigh and I kept expecting her to go off with someone she liked better, but she hasn't yet.

After we'd been mates for a while, I asked her why she was my friend. 'Don't you think I'm a bit quiet?' I asked.

'Not with me,' she said.

And it's true. Kayleigh is so good at having ideas and getting excited about things that it isn't hard for me to join in. I don't even mind being silly with Kayleigh because she's always much sillier and she never, ever laughs at me. She's also the only person I ever sing in front of. I haven't got an amazing, swoopy voice like Amelia, but I do like singing. Sometimes me and Kayleigh get dressed up like pop stars and borrow her mum's karaoke machine. I get the giggles a lot, but it's really good fun.

My other good friend is called Ashandra. I met her six months ago when I was at my dad's new house (we stay there every Wednesday night and every other weekend). Ashandra lives in the house next to his. One day I was sitting in the garden so that I didn't have to listen to Amelia shouting at Dad and Ashandra leant over the fence and said, 'How long have your parents been divorced for?' I thought that was a bit of a rude question, but then she told me about her parents splitting up and her mum getting married again and how her brother hates her stepdad. So she is quite an expert on divorce. Ashandra's also very smart and doesn't think I'm weird because maths is my favourite subject. She's tall (but not as tall as me) and she's always changing how she wears her curly Afro hair, but at the moment it's in lots of little plaits. She's also very understanding about missing your dad. Hers lives in America so she only sees him twice a year.

Ashandra and Kayleigh were both my special friends, but they hadn't actually met each other yet. When I found out that we were all going to be in the same tutor group when we went to St Mark's, I was really excited. I hoped that Ash and Kay would like each other and that we'd all be brilliant friends. It would be just like it was in London; I wouldn't ever care if someone was rude about my hair or my name or how tall I am because I'd always have a friend around.

I was also sort of hoping that, since this time I'd be starting school at the same time as everyone else, some other people in the class would be my friends too.

When we got to second helpings, I said, 'What's St Mark's like?'

Amelia crossed her eyes and stuck out her tongue. 'Music lessons are good; everything else sucks. That's all you need to know.'

Chloe scooped a large forkful of mash into her mouth. 'I'll tell you what's good about school: rugby, hockey, the doughnuts in the cafeteria – except don't eat the ones with sprinkles because my friend Thunder says that the dinner ladies put their toenail clippings on them to teach us a lesson for pushing so much in the queue.' She paused for more mash. 'And netball and rounders and the extra-long banisters in the languages block that you can slide down really fast.'

I'm not as keen on sport as Chloe is, but it all sounded quite fun.

'Is there anything not nice?' I asked.

'Lessons. But don't worry about that too much.'

'But it's lessons all the time.'

Chloe wrinkled her nose. 'Yeah, you have to be in the room, but you don't really have to pay that much attention.'

'I'm going to pretend I didn't hear that,' Mum said. 'Because I haven't got time to tell you how shocked I am and how I expect you to put more effort into your education. We'll have to save the lecture for when I can go back to not paying that much attention to my job.'

'I do listen in class,' Chloe protested. 'Just not all the time. Teachers always say things ten times anyway; you only need to listen once.'

Mum shook her head, but she was smiling a bit. She shut her laptop.

'Are you finished?' Lucy asked.

'I'll finish it when you're all in bed.' She turned

to me. 'You're not worried about school, are you, Ella?' she asked.

Worrying is the opposite of looking on the bright side so I shook my head. 'It'll be great being together with Ashandra and Kayleigh.'

'Remember it might take a while for everybody to adjust and get to know each other. And you're bound to make friends with other people in the class too.'

I pushed my peas round the plate. 'Do you think they'll like me?'

'Of course they will. Just be yourself.'

That sounded like good advice, but, after we'd finished and I went upstairs to look at my new uniform, the more I thought about it, the more worried I became. I mean, who exactly is myself? It's easy to say what my sisters are like. Amelia is cross and sarcastic and funny and tough. Chloe is thumping and gallumping and likes rugby and pudding. And Lucy is . . . well, there's nobody like Lucy. I bet she's never spent any time worrying about what she's like. She just is.

People love meeting my sisters. They like them. They remember them. I'm not quite so noticeable.

I trailed back downstairs to the kitchen. Chloe was doing the washing-up at the same time as eating a peanut butter and Marmite sandwich.

'Do you want one?' she asked.

'No thanks, I'm still full from tea.'

'Tell me if you change your mind. I'm going to do the next lot with chocolate spread as well as Marmite.'

'Chloe, what kind of person am I?' I asked.

'A nice one.'

'Anything else?'

'You're good at jumping.'

'What?'

'Remember when we played cricket with Dad and you made that catch?'

Then she said some nice stuff about me being kind, but mostly she went on about all the times that I haven't been terrible at sports so I gave up and went and tapped on Amelia's bedroom door.

'Come in if you've got me an answer to the torture of adolescence. Or lots of chocolate.'

I didn't have either of those things so I just said, 'Amelia, what am I like?' through the door.

There was a pause. Then the door opened.

'School's all right,' she said. 'It's pretty much the same as primary school, just bigger and with more people nagging you. Don't worry, people will like you. You're nice.'

I was surprised by this because mostly Amelia says I am a turbo idiot. 'Am I?'

'Yeah, if you tell any of the teachers apart from the music teacher that you're my sister, they'll probably be shocked that we're related because I'm revolting. You'll just have to give them time to get over the fact that you're not continuing the family tradition.'

She closed the door.

I asked Lucy next. She was in the sitting room, staring at the TV.

'Lucy, how would you describe me?'

'I wouldn't.'

'But if you had to?'

'I wouldn't because it would make noise and I don't want noise because I'm watching this magic show.'

I looked at the screen. A lady in a sparkly leotard was climbing into some sort of cabinet and the magician was waving a saw about. The mute sign was in the corner of the screen. 'You haven't even got the sound on,' I said.

'I know. The mysterious music is stupid. *Shh*.'

'Why do I have to *shh*?'

'Because I'm concentrating. I won't be able to remember how to do this on Saturday at ballet if you keep talking.'

'Just tell me how you would describe me and I'll—'

She put a hand over my mouth, then, without taking her eyes off the TV, she picked up a magazine and a pen from the coffee table. She wrote something and handed it to me.

There was one word written in her large, wobbly handwriting:

NICE

I let her go back to the magic.

Mrs Bottomley always said that 'nice' was a wishy-washy word that didn't really mean anything and that we weren't allowed to use it in our writing.

But nice is better than horrible. I'm not ultra-clever like Amelia, or amazingly chatty like Chloe, or even adorably crazy like Lucy, but maybe if I was super nice people would notice me and like me.

CHAPTER ♥ FOUR

On Monday morning when I got up, I couldn't find my new school skirt, even though I had very carefully clipped it on to one of those special skirt hangers as soon as I got it. In the end, I found it in the bathroom. It was being a tent for Lucy's Action Man. Back in our bedroom, Chloe was still in bed, but Lucy was dancing around naked.

'Lucy!' I said. 'Can you please not use my skirt?'

'Not use it for what?'

'Not for anything! I need it for wearing.'

Lucy made a grumbly noise. 'I never get new skirts. Why do you always get new things?' She pulled her old gingham school dress over her head. 'I get things that Amelia has worn and then Chloe has worn. And when Chloe wears things she makes them stink.'

'I think that dress has been washed since Chloe wore it.'

Lucy gave me a look. 'Yes, but I still *know* what she did in it.'

Chloe pulled her duvet off her face. 'Are you saying the ghost of my farts lives on in those dresses? Cool.'

Lucy yanked her socks on. 'It's very not cool. And I won't ever wear the dress that you used the skirt to carry frogspawn in.'

Chloe tumbled out of the top bunk. 'Mum will make you.'

'She can't. It's not here any more.'

I exchanged a look with Chloe. 'Where is it, Lucy?'

'I'm not telling you. If I tell you then I'll have to bury you in the same place.'

I hoped that Mum wouldn't find out about the dress because, when people do things to clothes that Cost Good Money, Mum gets mad about possessions not being properly looked after and made the most of, and it usually ends up in a Complete Sort Out.

A Complete Sort Out means you have to take everything out of your wardrobe and drawers and you are only allowed to put back the things that are clean and neat and fit you. You are not allowed to keep old school projects, even if you did use half a packet of pipe cleaners on them, and, before the inspection, you have to remember to hide your old birthday cards from when they said 'love Mum and Dad' on the same card.

Lucy was hopping towards the door, but Chloe grabbed her by the elbow. 'Don't let Mum find out about the dress or she'll be mad.'

That wasn't a very clever thing to say to Lucy because, even when someone else might be cross, Lucy is always crosser.

'I'm not going to! And I wouldn't have to bury things or chop things up or post them in the postbox if everybody just gave me what I want.'

I know the things that Lucy wants. She keeps a list on our noticeboard. It includes: 'no more traffic lights' and 'a really nice axe'.

I don't think we should give her what she wants.

'Anyway,' Chloe said, 'Ella has to have new things because she's so ginormous.' She meant it in a kind way, but the word 'ginormous' is only really nice when you're talking about cakes or trampolines.

I'm not ginormous fat, just ginormous tall. None of Amelia's old things fit me because I'm already taller than her.

By the time we got downstairs, Mum was at the

why-ing stage. When we're late, which is always, Mum has three stages. She starts out with hurrying and saying things like, 'Please stop singing into that hairbrush and sort your hair out, Chloe.' Then she gets to why-ing where she stomps about, looking for things she needs for work, and saying, 'Why is there a face flannel under the table? Why has my diary got ketchup all over it?' The last stage is when she turns into one of those army men and just barks out orders. She got to the army stage when Amelia finally appeared in the kitchen, smoothing down her fringe while reading her poetry book.

'Everybody move!' Mum snapped.

'But w—' Lucy started.

'Lunches,' Mum said, pointing to four Tupperware boxes on the counter.

'An—' Chloe began.

'Shoes,' said Mum and pointed into the hall.

I opened my mouth to say I was hungry.

'Magic Breakfast,' Mum said. 'Line up!'

Magic Breakfast started when Lucy began nursery and Mum first went back to work. We all stand in the kitchen, holding a glass, and Mum pours milk into each one. (If we hold the glasses close together, she can do it in one long pour across the top without spilling a drop.) Then you've got about fifteen seconds to drink your milk. During that time, Mum hands you a pack of mini cereal and you eat the cereal while walking to school. The magic is that the milk and the cereal combine in your tummy just like a proper sit-down bowl of breakfast.

'This isn't very magic any more' Lucy said, wiping her milk moustache on Chloe's sleeve.

'You're just saying that because I got the Frosties,' Chloe said, wiping her own milk moustache on her sleeve.

'The magic is that I get to work on time,' Mum said, picking up a bag of books and a stack of paper. Then she noticed Amelia trying to slip back upstairs. 'Door! Now, now, now!'

'I don't know why you're complaining,' Chloe said to Lucy. 'You get another meal at Breakfast Club anyway. Why can't we go to Breakfast Club, Mum? They do actually have one at our school. People get to go inside in the warm and eat toast; the rest of us have to skulk about outside.'

'Skulking is cheaper.' Mum bustled us out of the door. 'Besides, it's a skill for life. Look at the good use Amelia has put her skulking skills to already.' She slammed the door behind us. 'Everybody got everything?'

'I seem to have misplaced my will to live,' Amelia said.

'Always the last place you look,' Mum said and she gave us a kiss that was a bit like the milk pouring – it slid across all four of us in one go. 'Good luck, Ella. Hope you have a lovely first day.' Then she scooped Lucy into the car and drove off.

Amelia sighed loudly and pulled out a tiny mirror and the eyeliner that she's not supposed to wear to school and drew dark rings round her eyes. She gave us both a half-hearted wave before striding off.

'Do you want to walk with me and Thunder?' Chloe asked me.

I swallowed a mouthful of dry cornflakes. 'No, I said I'd call for Kayleigh.'

'Do you remember where you're going from your induction day?'

I nodded. I did remember and also, when we visited for our induction day in July, I made a little map of the school just in case I suddenly forgot. It was in my sock. Just in case I lost my bag.

Chloe gave me a friendly punch on the arm. 'If you have any problems, just ask someone to find me. Everybody knows me.'

Kayleigh lives three streets away. When I rang the bell, her mum opened the door.

'Hiya, Ella.' She turned her head and shouted, 'Kayleigh! Ella's here. Get a move on!' She was wearing those funny sticking-out trousers ready for her job at the stables. Kayleigh and her mum are both mad about horses. They've been saving up to buy their own horse the whole time I've known Kayleigh.

Kayleigh came out of the kitchen, carrying her new bag. Her mum kissed her on the cheek.

'Bye, babe, have a good day. Don't let the big kids give you any nonsense.'

I wanted to ask her what sort of nonsense she thought the big kids might give us, but she kissed Kayleigh again and pushed us out of the door.

'I can't wait,' Kayleigh said. 'Can you? Now we're not babies any more and there's going to be a proper art room, not just loads of pots with the paint all dried up in them.'

She didn't stop talking for the whole twenty minutes it took us to walk to school. She was really excited about the cafeteria and the art teacher and having an actual upstairs at school. And she thought we should ask our mums if we could wear nail varnish now we were in Year Seven.

She didn't pay any attention to the traffic. I think that's another reason why we're good at being friends. I make sure that Kayleigh doesn't get run over and she's so excited all the time that she helps me remember the bright sides of things.

When we walked in the gates of St Mark's, there were already tons of kids hanging about.

'Some of them are really grown up,' I said in a low voice.

Kayleigh looked up at me (she's nearly a whole head shorter than I am so she's always looking up). 'Ella, you're grown up.'

'I'm not. I'm tall, but I'm still quite little.'

We managed to find our registration room. When we got there, Ashandra was already sitting at a table. Somehow, she made the school uniform look really cool and, even though she didn't get to go to the induction day because she was in America visiting her dad, she looked completely not nervous. You can just tell by looking at some people's faces that they don't have any secret maps in their socks.

'Ash!' I called, waving to her. 'This is Kayleigh.' I'd told them so much about each other that I'd imagined them hugging when they met. But they didn't hug; instead, they looked at each other like you do when someone shows you their dog and you don't know if you should stroke it because it might not be friendly.

Then Ash smiled. 'I got us this table,' she said.

The tables were arranged in four columns. Each one had two chairs neatly tucked behind. 'We just need another chair.'

I hesitated. It seemed like someone had arranged the classroom exactly how they wanted it, but Kayleigh grabbed a chair from the next table and plonked herself down in it.

Lots more people arrived and everyone looked at everyone else in their stiff new uniforms.

Then the bell rang and the door flew open and in walked our teacher. Her black hair was even curlier than I remembered and she was wearing a dress the colour of poppies.

'Ooof,' she said, dropping a pile of books on the desk. 'Being new is terrible, isn't it? Terrible.'

She flopped into her chair and rifled through a pile of papers.

'She needs to go on a diet,' whispered a girl sitting across the aisle. She was wearing the high-heeled shoes that Mum wouldn't let Amelia buy. Her friend giggled.

'She's even got fat *knees*.'

That wasn't true, but her friend giggled again.

'In case you've forgotten, my name is Miss Espinoza. I teach Spanish and also French and I'm your tutor. Remember, I am just like you; this school is new for me too. In July, we came for the day to meet each other and now it is our first proper day together. So nobody in this room knows what they are doing or where they are going.' She said it in such a happy way that twenty-eight pairs of shoulders relaxed a bit.

'We will work it out,' she said. 'We will help each other. If you see someone trying to have a French lesson in the swimming pool then you must whisper in their ear. And that includes me.'

There were a few giggles.

'Be nice to each other,' she said.

I smiled because that was exactly what I was planning to do. Maybe even Miss Espinoza would notice how super nice I was.

She took a good look at our table. I sat very still.

'Girls,' she said to me, Kayleigh and Ashandra. 'One of you needs to move over here.' She pointed to a table across the aisle that had one lonely girl sitting behind it. 'Then we're all two to a table. Yes?'

Kayleigh looked at me. We had all agreed to sit together. I didn't want to move, but I really did want Ash and Kay to have the chance to get to know each other. I'd promised myself I'd be nice and I supposed that meant doing difficult things sometimes so I moved my chair across the aisle to sit next to the girl. She had her hair pulled back in a tight plait with a fuzz of frizz escaping around her face. She didn't look at me when I sat down.

'Thank you. Now we have to find the register on here.' Miss Espinoza flipped open her laptop.

After registration, we went to maths. First, we had a test so the teacher could work out what level we are at. There were some groans, but I quite liked it because in maths I always know what to do. I didn't know what to do when someone shouted, 'Look at lamp-post girl!' as we were moving to our next lesson so I didn't do anything.

In RE, we filled in a questionnaire and played a game. It was two chairs to a table again so, to be nice, I suggested Ashandra and Kayleigh sit together. I was next to a boy because he was last to arrive and the only space left was beside me. He didn't say a single word the whole time. And I ended up behind the girl who'd called Miss Espinoza fat. Her friend called her Jasmine. All the way through RE she made rude comments about how gross our teacher's tie was. I kept sneaking looks at Ashandra and Kayleigh to see how they were getting on, but there wasn't really a chance for them to get friendly. Everybody was being first-day quiet. Even Kieran from my primary school was sitting still and pretending not to be a nightmare.

'Playtime!' I said when RE was finished.

High Heels Jasmine turned round to face me and laughed. 'It's called *break*. This isn't primary school.' And she looked at me as if she knew that I'd still got some Sylvanian Families under my bed.

'She can call it what she wants,' Kayleigh said to Jasmine, linking arms with me and leading me off outside. This is exactly why I'm so glad I've got my friends at school with me. I just freeze when people are mean, but Kayleigh and Ashandra know exactly what to do.

After breaktime (where no one does any playing and you have to be careful where you stand because someone in Year Ten might want to stand there), it was time for double PE.

I came out of the changing room in my super-white new trainers and the PE teacher looked at me and smiled. 'You look like you'll do well this morning,' she said as she opened a net of basketballs.

The bright side of being tall is that I can reach things from the top shelf and it's better to be called 'giraffe' than 'elephant'. Another bright side, which I found out in PE, is that after you've been picked first for a basketball team and disappointed everyone then snooty girls with heels promise you that they're never going to make that mistake again.

The rest of the day took a long time to be over. I kept trying to be nice and say that Ashleigh and

Kayleigh could sit together in our classes so they could get to know each other, but they didn't seem to want to. And at lunchtime I ended up having two different conversations, even though I wanted to get us all talking together.

When I got home, Chloe and Amelia were already back, but Lucy has to go to After School Club and wait for Mum to pick her up because she's too little to be at home alone with us. I was going to have a drink, but I suddenly felt really tired so I lay down on the sofa, just for a minute.

But in our house, if you lie down and close your eyes, people jump on you.

When Chloe had finished her trampoline routine, I sat up and pulled the hair out of my mouth.

'You're all red,' Chloe said. 'Did you have a disgusting day at school?'

'I'm red because you just did a somersault on my head.'

'What about school?'

'It was OK. I mean, some of it was nice.' I wanted to tell her a list of nice things, but I hadn't made one yet. 'It was jam sponge for pudding.'

'I know. I had three lots. Your face is quite crumply. Like an elephant. Or a bulldog. Are you going to cry?'

'Dad says crying is for babies.'

'Crying is for anyone who feels like it. Like farting.' She squeezed my shoulder.

I don't know why Amelia says Chloe is dumb. She says some smart things to me.

'I'll make you a sandwich,' she said.

The sandwich had three types of cheese and two types of pickle in it.

Even if a sandwich is disgusting, if it was meant in a very kind way, it can still make you feel better.

CHAPTER ❤ FIVE

When Mum and Lucy got home, Mum had a huge box of doughnuts for us.

The bright side of having a mum who's a teacher is the food. Bringing home doughnuts is not unusual. And at Christmas and Easter and the summer holidays Mum gets lots of boxes of chocolates which she shares with us. On special picnic days and party days and bring-and-share lunch days, there's always lots left over and Mum brings us something home. There's more food in schools than you'd think.

'The head bought them for the teachers,' Mum said.

'Why?' Lucy asked. 'Nobody gave me a doughnut at school. We did halving today. Halving is hard; I should get a doughnut for that.'

'Mum works much harder than you do. Anyway, you're having a doughnut now,' Amelia pointed out.

'Yes, but it wasn't meant for me. It's a second-hand doughnut.'

'It's not really second hand,' I said. 'Because no one else has had a go at it first. If they had, it would be all chewed.'

'Like this,' Chloe said and she opened her mouth to show us.

'Why exactly did the head give you doughnuts?' Amelia asked Mum.

'Because he's trying to bribe us all into doing what he wants and not to complain about stress and the broken toilets.'

Chloe put two more doughnuts on her fingers like rings. 'But there are loads here. Didn't anyone eat them?'

Mum shook her head. 'No one wanted him to think that they were agreeing.'

'I wouldn't get stressed if someone gave me a doughnut every day,' Chloe said.

'You never get stressed about anything or anyone anyway,' Amelia said.

Mum filled up the kettle. 'Well, I've heard a whisper that we might be inspected this term so the head's going to need some pretty big doughnuts if he thinks he can stop us from getting stressed.'

'Will it be Daddy that inspectors you?' Lucy asked.

My mum and dad used to work at the same school, but then Mum had lots of children and stayed at home to look after us while my dad got more and more important until he was head teacher and then he stopped being a head and became an inspector instead.

'No,' Mum said with a funny look on her face. 'Dad won't inspect my school; he doesn't work in this area.'

Lucy twirled one of her coppery curls round a sugary finger. 'If inspectors are so evil, why is Daddy one?'

'Because obviously Dad could never do anything evil,' Amelia said.

She was being sarcastic, which is Amelia's favourite pastime and is basically saying the opposite to what you mean.

Mum was staring into the tea bag tin.

'Duh,' Chloe said. 'Dad's not one of the evil ones. He's a good one.'

Lucy was happy with that, but I saw Amelia raising her eyebrows at Mum. I didn't know what it meant except that Amelia doesn't think that my dad is very good. But Amelia doesn't think anyone is very good at the moment. Mum says she'll grow out of it eventually.

I hope it's before Christmas.

'But you are going to be inspected by someone?' Chloe asked Mum.

'Quite possibly. It's been a while since they last came to our school so we're definitely due a visit. But nobody knows for certain.'

'That's rude,' Lucy said. 'You should send them one of those bits that you get on party invitations that says "yes, I am coming" or "no, I wouldn't come to your stinky party even if you paid me".'

Mum fished the tea bag out of her cup. 'It doesn't work like that. They used to tell you when they were coming so that you could work yourself up to a nervous breakdown. Then they said they'd only give you a few days' notice so that you had to squeeze all your panicking into a weekend, but now they just turn up and you get to go insane right in front of them.'

'What does "just turn up" mean?' Lucy asked.

'It means they can strike at any time,' I said.

'Like zombies,' Chloe added.

'Does that mean you've got a lot of work to do?' Amelia asked.

Mum frowned. 'Let's forget about work tonight. How about after tea we get into our pyjamas and watch a film and eat some popcorn?'

My mum doesn't have to try to be nice, she just is.

Talking about zombies must have put ideas in Chloe's head because, while Mum was listening to the news and making our tea, Chloe convinced us all to play March of the Zombies.

We have lots of made-up games in our family. Amelia won't play most of them any more, but sometimes you can talk her into March of the Zombies. She says it appeals to the apocalypse in her soul.

I think that means she likes the biting.

Our house has a basement, which is really good because when you make a lot of noise down there it sounds like slightly less noise up at ground level.

When we moved into this house, the basement had pale blue walls and a wooden floor painted white, and Mum and Dad said it was going to be the playroom. After three weeks, everyone was calling it the Pit.

Our house has quite a lot of clutter in it, but the Pit seems especially full because it's where all the tiny things live. Like Lego bricks and Barbie shoes and felt-tip-pen lids and Playmobil people. They fill up the Pit as if a plastic monster has done a multicoloured plastic sick all over the floor.

Underneath all the tiny stuff, the floor isn't white any more. Now it's covered in paint and dried-on Play-Doh and some brown sticky stuff that no one can identify. Even the walls aren't empty because once, when Lucy was bored, she decided to put some stories on them. She couldn't write then so she just drew pictures. There are a lot of people shouting and fighting.

I don't really like mess. I keep my corner of our bedroom very neat and always try to keep my bits and bobs tidied away. But the Pit does look as if something evil has smashed everything up so I guess it's a good place to play zombies. Especially because there's no window down there and you can make it properly dark.

'I'm too old for this,' Amelia said, but she closed the door and turned off the light anyway.

'I'll be the zombie,' I said because I was still trying to be nice and nobody ever volunteers to go first. I positioned myself with my back against the door, counted to three and then started to walk slowly across the room with my arms stretched out to the sides, trying to be as quiet as possible, which is quite hard when you're stepping on bits of board games and something squidgy. When my fingers brushed someone's hair, I made a grab. 'I'll eat your brains!' I said and gave the victim a very gentle bite. (When we first started playing, the bites were much harder, but one of the neighbours complained to Mum about the blood-curdling screams coming from our house.) I could tell from the tiny shoulders that I'd caught Lucy, that and the way she muttered, 'It's so unfair,' because the rules said that Lucy was now a zombie too.

After a few minutes, I found Chloe which meant Amelia was the last person left and when we found her we lifted her up high and proclaimed her the zombie queen.

Even though she tried not to smile, I think she liked it.

She switched on the light. 'Must be nice being a zombie,' she said.

Chloe poked her. 'You'd know.'

Amelia pinched her back. 'I don't know why people are always running away from them in films. If the zombies come, I'm not going to wear myself out trying to escape. I'll just give in and become one of them.'

'But your brain would be zombified. You wouldn't be able to think. Don't you want to use your brain?' Lucy said, looking shocked.

'You sound like my science teacher.'

Lucy's eyes were wide. 'It's not just no thinking:

it takes away everything. If a zombie bit me, I wouldn't be Lucy any more.'

We all laughed because not being Lucy is the worst possible thing that Lucy can imagine.

'Anyway, I'll leave you *babies* to your games. I've got things to discuss with Mum,' Amelia said, opening the door. 'I'm just saying it would be nice not to think about stuff sometimes.'

Ashandra and Kayleigh sitting silently next to each other at lunch popped into my mind.

I knew what Amelia meant.

CHAPTER ❤ SIX

The bright side of Wednesdays is that when it's finished you're more than halfway through the school week. And I get to go to my dad's after school.

I had been trying really hard to be nice and to get Ash and Kay to be nice to each other as well. They had been nice, but I was worried that it was *too* nice. They said things like, 'Please can I borrow your green pen? Or, 'I like your headband,' but they never said, 'Give me a crisp before you scoff them all,' or, 'Budge up, big bum'. Chloe says things like that to me all the time. And Chloe really likes me.

But I started to hope that things were progressing in our music lesson before lunch on Wednesday.

The tables in the music room are in long rows

and that means three people can sit together. I had Ashandra on one side and Kayleigh on the other. Ash was doing an impression of her choir leader accidentally smacking himself in the face with a tambourine and we were all cracking up. This was how I had always imagined things and I hoped that it was the beginning of the three of us being best friends forever.

When I looked up to make sure Mr O'Brien hadn't noticed us laughing, I saw that it was only two minutes to lunchtime and the music room was a complete mess.

Even though it was only my third day, I'd already realised that there are basically two types of teacher at secondary school. One lot start getting you packed up before it's time for the lesson to finish. They make sure everything is exactly in its place and then you have to sit down and answer questions about what you've learnt so that everybody knows that you've done some learning, even if what you mostly remember about the lesson is that Kieran tried to climb out of the window. When the bell goes, those kinds of teachers let you file out tidily. I think the other lot of teachers missed the day of training when you learn about filing out tidily because they carry on doing stuff right until the bell rings and, when it does, they look really surprised as if they thought you were all just going to keep on learning about S-bend rivers forever. They start shouting about things you need to tidy up and homework you have to do, but most people aren't listening because they're edging towards the door and Kieran has already got his crisps out.

Mr O'Brien is one of those surprised-by-the-bell ones. When the bell went, his head snapped up and he said, 'Remember to listen out for examples of the twelve-bar blues!' and started hurling tambourines back on their hooks in the cupboard. Half the class were on their feet before he turned round and saw that the tables were covered in singing books.

'Who's going to be really kind and put away the books?' he asked.

If you're not being nice, you can pretend you haven't heard a teacher saying something like that because putting away your pencil case is making too much noise. But I was being nice so I raised my hand.

'Thank you, Ella.' With that, Mr O'Brien scooted out of the door and almost everyone else followed him.

'I'll help you,' Kayleigh said.

'No, *I'll* help you,' Ashandra said and she gave

Kayleigh a glare like we'd never laughed about her choir leader getting a jingly bit up his nose at all.

I didn't want them to glare at each other.

'Why don't you two just go to lunch?' I said quickly.

'Are you sure?' Kay asked.

I nodded.

I thought they'd go off to queue up together and save me a seat, but when they went out of the door I could see through the window that Ashandra ran to catch up with a girl called Erica and Kayleigh didn't bother to follow.

Then I realised that not only were there books all over the tables, they were all over the floor too.

The bright side about getting to the cafeteria when all the ham sandwiches have already gone is that soggy salad ones are 10p cheaper.

After lunch, Ashandra walked to geography with Erica and when they sat down together I didn't even try to get a table for me and Kayleigh behind them. But, as we walked in, Kayleigh noticed me watching Ashandra laughing with Erica.

'I don't know why you like her so much,' Kayleigh said, dropping her geography book on the table. 'She's so lah-di-dah.'

I stared at Kayleigh. 'What do you mean?' I asked.

'You know, she's got a lah-di-dah voice and I bet she lives in a big house.'

'Why does it matter how big her house is?'

'It doesn't. But she's always using long words and she said, "I can't believe you've got your ears pierced!"'

'Maybe it was in a wow-you're-so-lucky-I-can't-believe-it way,' I said, trying to squish the funny feeling in my tummy.

'It wasn't. She told me her mum says she doesn't understand why girls mutilate themselves like that.'

'Ash's mum says millions of things. She just wants girls to be equal to boys.'

'I can wear earrings and be equal to boys,' Kayleigh said and rolled her eyes. 'Anyway, half of them have got earrings too.'

'I suppose so. Listen, if you get to know Ash, I think you'll really like her. She's dead funny. She was funny in music this morning, wasn't she?'

Kayleigh shrugged.

'Hey, sometimes me and Ashandra make funny videos on her phone. Shall we ask her if she wants to do one after school?' I had been looking forward to seeing my dad, but I really wanted Ash and Kay to spend time together.

Kayleigh shook her head. 'I said I'd help my mum at the stables.'

I was trying so hard to be nice and make sacrifices to bring them together, but it didn't seem to be working. I was starting to think that maybe Mrs Bottomley was right and 'nice' didn't really mean anything much at all.

CHAPTER ❦ SEVEN

When the bell went at the end of the day, I walked back to my dad's house with Ashandra.

'What do you think of school so far?' I asked.

'It's pretty good. I like moving round to different lessons; it's better than being with one teacher all day.'

'I like Miss Espinoza too,' I said.

'She's nice. And I like Mr Garibaldi and Mrs Holt is a really good teacher. The lessons are more interesting than primary school, aren't they?' She smiled.

'Yes, I suppose so.' I didn't smile.

'Ella! Stop pretending you're not super smart. You don't need to worry about schoolwork.'

'I'm not worrying,' I said. 'I mean, I think maybe Mrs Holt thought that thing I said about book blurbs was silly.'

'Mrs Holt can see that you're clever and nice. All the teachers think that, except maybe the scary ones, because when you try to answer their questions you go really quiet and they can't actually hear that you're giving them the right answer. You just look like this to them.' She opened and shut her mouth like a bashful goldfish.

'Hey!'

'It's all right. You look very intelligent while you're doing it so they probably give you the benefit of the doubt.'

I couldn't help laughing.

Ash grinned. 'Don't worry, we'll get used to all the new teachers and we've got loads of cool stuff coming up. That author project is going to be fun.'

I'm not crazy about doing projects, but I was pleased that Mrs Holt said we could choose our own groups. Most teachers like to tell you who to be with in a group. I think they think you can't be happy and do work at the same time so they put you in a horrible group so you just work and work because you don't want to speak to people who don't like you.

'I guess so,' I said. 'Which author shall we do for our project?'

Ash looked away. 'Um . . . I haven't really decided yet.'

'We should probably wait till tomorrow to talk about it anyway so we can ask Kayleigh who she wants to do.'

'Maybe.'

It was the kind of 'maybe' that Mum says when Lucy asks if she can have a power drill for her birthday.

'Don't you want to work with us?' I asked.

Ashandra twisted the strap of her bag. 'I don't know. I think people are more efficient when they work in pairs. And you know how much I love being efficient – nearly as much I love telling people the best way to *be* efficient.'

'Oh.' I tried not to look upset. It was time to try being nice again. 'Well, it's OK if you and Kayleigh work together.'

'Actually, I've sort of already asked Erica to work with me.'

I couldn't see how we were all going to be best friends if Ashandra and Kayleigh didn't even spend any time together, but I didn't say anything.

When Amelia let me into Dad's house, she looked unusually cheerful. 'Lucy's arguing with the Ice Queen,' she grinned.

My stomach clenched. I'm not keen on arguments and I would never dare argue with Suvi; she's got quite a stern face.

Amelia disappeared upstairs, probably to text Mum about the fight, and I hovered in the doorway to the kitchen. Lucy was staring at Suvi with her hands on her hips. 'But why don't you have a TV?' she asked.

Lucy starts this argument almost every time we go to Dad's. I don't know why she won't let it go.

Suvi was very calmly slicing leeks. I think it's her calmness that scares me a bit. Everybody in our family gets very worked up about arguments. But Suvi just stays the same. Amelia says it's because she has no real emotions.

Baby Kirsti was in a basket on legs looking at the ceiling. Chloe was sitting at the kitchen table, eating a packet of crisps and watching the argument instead of the television. I don't know where she got the crisps. The only snack that Suvi has ever given me is rice cakes. It's like eating polystyrene.

Suvi dropped the chopped leeks in a saucepan. 'Television is not good for your imagination,' she said.

Lucy widened her eyes. 'Haven't you ever watched any TV? It's full of imagination.'

'I think that it is better for you to use your own imagination.'

Lucy flopped her head about. 'I already had to

use my imagination all day at school because there's no TV there either.'

'I'm surprised that your mother approves. She's an educator, yes? There is research that shows television has a negative influence on children's mood and concentration.'

TV isn't the only difference between our house and Dad's. At home it's not just the Pit that is crammed full of things. Everywhere you look there's stuff; plates in the sink, dirty clothes spilling out of the laundry bin, Lucy's toys on the floor. We haven't even got enough shelves for all our books so there's a giant wobbly structure in the corner of the sitting room called Book Mountain.

Dad's house is more . . . empty. There are big bits of white space everywhere. Some of their shelves have only got one vase on. The walls are white and the chairs and sofas and other furniture are white too, or grey or beige. Dad says it's calming. Chloe says it's boring. Amelia says it's pretentious, which is when you have silly stuff because you think it makes you look good. But actually I think Suvi really likes it. She prefers things to be simple. I've never seen her wear anything spotty or flowery.

Suvi started telling Lucy about the percentage of children who do horrible things after they've been watching TV. I sat down at the table next to Chloe.

'How was your day?' I asked.

'Stupid. Some of the girls in my class have started wearing that black stuff on their eyes like Amelia.'

'Oh.'

'I mean, if I wanted to dress up like a vampire, I might draw black circles round my eyes, but I don't know why they think it makes them look cool.'

'Me neither.'

'They reckon it will make the boys want to kiss them.'

'Does it?'

Chloe screwed up her face. 'Dunno. Why would you want a gross boy to kiss you anyway? They're all stupid.'

I nodded. 'Where's Dad?'

Our dad is supposed to finish early on Wednesdays so that he can get home to spend time with us, but often he gets tied up with writing reports and other important things.

'He rang,' Chloe said. 'He said he's r—'

'Running late,' I finished.

'Yep. But he'll be back by five and he said he'll take us to the cinema to see that film we've been pestering him about.'

I love the cinema. Sitting in the dark with lots of people and the bigness of the screen and the loudness of the loud bits makes the whole film more intense.

Chloe and me watched Lucy and Suvi saying the same things that they always say when they argue about TV, then I did my history homework. When it was ten to five, I looked at Suvi. Even though I'd known her for over a year, I still hadn't quite got used to her. I expected her to tell us it was time to get ready, but Suvi doesn't really do that sort of thing.

'Lucy,' I said, trying to take charge. 'You need to put your shoes on.'

'I don't like those shoes.'

'But you've got to wear shoes so we can go to the cinema.'

Lucy squeezed her eyes half shut and glowered at me. I hate it when she does that.

'Ah,' said Chloe. 'Lucy's giving you the evil eye!'

'I'm just trying to help you get ready,' I said to Lucy. 'And you'd better go to the loo before we leave.'

Lucy's eyes narrowed to slits.

'Oh, she's good!' Chloe said. 'I've taught her well.'

Obviously, Chloe wasn't going to be any help. 'Suvi, Lucy won't go to the loo,' I said.

'So?'

'Can you make her?'

'I cannot make her.'

Lucy stopped evil-eyeing me and smiled.

I turned back to Suvi. 'But what if she needs to go in the middle of the film?'

'Then she will miss some.'

Lucy doesn't like missing things. 'What if she just wets herself in the cinema?'

'Then I think people will say, "Look at that little girl. She has peed."'

Lucy's scowl came back, but I noticed that, when Suvi went to check on her saucepan, Lucy crept upstairs to the bathroom.

At twenty past five, we heard Dad's car pull into the driveway.

A few moments later, he opened the front door and called, 'I'm here! Don't panic. Everybody ready?'

Chloe gave him a bear hug and started telling him about how many goals she'd scored in netball.

'Lucy still hasn't put on her shoes,' I told him.

'Lucy, put your shoes on. We're going to miss the beginning if we don't leave now.'

'I can't. I haven't got any socks on.'

'Where are your socks?'

'Chloe's wearing them.'

'Is that right, Clo?'

'They were clean. Well, cleanish. My ones were all muddy.'

'What's Lucy supposed to wear?'

'I don't know. I'm not Lucy.'

'Showing your usual consideration for others,' Amelia said to Chloe, pushing past her to grab her own shoes.

'Take these.' Suvi handed Lucy a balled-up pair of socks.

'Are those baby socks? Because I'm not a baby. I'm seven. I can swim twenty-five metres.'

'They're your socks; you left them last time you were here.'

Lucy put on the socks and shoes and we scrambled out of the door.

'What time does it start?' Dad asked.

'Three and a half minutes ago,' Amelia said. She sounded a little bit pleased.

'Can we get there in time?' Lucy asked.

'Not without a time machine,' Dad said.

'How long does it take to drive there?' Chloe asked.

'Ten minutes.'

'If you drive really fast, you can get there three and a half minutes ago, can't you, Dad?'

'I'll see what I can do, Lucy.' He pulled open the back door of the car. 'Oh . . .'

'Poo,' Chloe said.

'Don't say poo,' Lucy said. 'You're not supposed to say poo. Why is poo a bad word, Daddy? Is it because poo stinks? Is it? And poo is disgusting?'

'Stop saying poo, Lucy,' I said.

Dad was staring at Kirsti's car seat which was taking up a whole person-sized space in the back seat.

'Doesn't that come out?' Amelia asked.

'The base is screwed in. It'll take a while for me to get it undone.' There was only room for four people in the car and there were five of us including Dad.

'Could Lucy sit in it?' Chloe asked.

Lucy's eyes blazed. 'I —'

Dad put his hand over her mouth before she could start lecturing us about how seven-year-olds are practically grown up and don't sit in baby car seats.

'She needs to sit on her own booster seat anyway,' Dad said.

'We're missing all the trailers,' Chloe whined.

'I could stay here,' I said quietly. But it doesn't count as being nice if no one can hear you so I said it a bit louder.

'Really, Ella?' Dad asked.

Amelia was already getting into the car.

'Do you want me to stay with you?' Chloe asked.

'That's OK,' I said. I did want her to stay, but we'd seen the trailer for the film and there were lots of people walking into things and one bit where someone jumped out of a car as it fell off a bridge. Those are things that Chloe really likes in a film.

They all got into the car and I watched them drive away. It seemed pretty unfair that Kirsti was taking my place, even though she wasn't actually in the car. But it's not very bright side-ish to think mean things about a baby so I stopped staring at where the car had been and went back into the house.

Suvi was breastfeeding Kirsti. When I told her what had happened, she said, 'Do you want me to drive you? Kirsti has just started, but when she is finished I can take you.'

Suvi had already explained to us that Kirsti's feeds weren't in a pattern yet and sometimes she feeds for ages.

'No. It's OK,' I said.

'It was kind of you to let your sisters go,' she said.

Which was nice because none of the people I was being kind to seemed to have noticed.

'I've just made a pot of peppermint tea; do you want to get yourself some?' she asked.

I didn't, but I went to the kitchen and poured a cup anyway.

I'd never really spent any time alone with Suvi. I wished it was Dad I was with because I didn't often get to talk to him alone. I slurped my tea for something to do. It wasn't very tea-ish. Or even very pepperminty. We used to make potions out of leaves in the back garden and once Chloe persuaded me to drink a mouthful, even though I was afraid we'd poison ourselves. The peppermint tea tasted a bit like the leaf potion.

I wondered if they'd missed much of the film.

'At least Lucy won't need to pee,' I said.

Suvi nodded. 'Lucy does not like to be told what to do, yes?'

I don't think I've ever seen Lucy follow an instruction, but it didn't seem right to be talking about her like that with Suvi so I just said, 'I think she finds it difficult, you know, being at home and then being here.'

'Of course. Change is unsettling.'

I nodded. 'I guess she thought . . . *we* thought that we knew about our family and then it's a bit of

a surprise when you suddenly get an extra person.'
Kirsti flailed a tiny arm. 'Two extra people.'

There was a pause.

'Yes, I can see that having extra people is hard,'
Suvi said.

I was watching her face carefully because when
someone is feeding a baby it seems rude to look
at their boob. I had always thought that Suvi had
a face with no feelings in it and a voice that was
serious all the time. But, when I looked at her,
there was a bit of a joke in her eyes. I wasn't sure
what the joke was to start with, but then I realised
that she had suddenly got *four* more people in her
family. And one of them was Lucy. And another
was Amelia. I felt bad for Suvi because I'd never
even wondered what it felt like to suddenly have
four stepchildren.

'My mum says that people take a while to get
used to each other,' I said.

'Your mother is smart.'

I knew that, but I hadn't expected Suvi to know
it too. I couldn't think of a time when Mum and
Suvi had even really been in the same room.

Suvi tucked a cushion behind her back. 'Your
dad and I really would like for you girls to feel at
home here,' she said.

It was a nice thing to say. I couldn't tell her that

I couldn't ever imagine us trampolining on the sofa or having a floor picnic like we do at home.

'Lucy would be happier with a TV,' I said.

Suvi sighed. 'You have to remember that it is also my home and Kirsti's home and your father's too. I want my family, all my family, to talk and play, not to watch TV.'

It seemed like she really felt strongly about that. I tried to think of something smaller that would make Lucy happy.

'How about orange squash? Would it not be your home with squash in it?'

Normally, you only got water to drink at Dad's house. Or leaf-potion tea.

Suvi tilted her head to one side. 'I guess I can handle some squash,' she said. 'I'll keep the door of the cupboard closed so I don't have to look at its sugariness.'

Her eyes were joking again.

I sipped my tea very slowly until Kirsti finished feeding. She was so full that while Suvi was winding her she went off to sleep. Suvi laid her gently in her basket.

'I'm going to send some work emails now, OK?' she asked.

'Are they making you do work already? I thought you were having your maternity time off?'

'I am. I won't go back to work until the summer, but I'm trying to keep in touch. I want to see how my projects are going. They can probably do them without me, but I like to think they can't.'

I had finished all my homework so I looked at the algebra chapter in my maths textbook. I like algebra because you start off with a mystery number, but if you follow the rules you can work out what it is. It's like detective work.

After a long while, Suvi put some papers back in a file and shut her laptop and asked me, 'Do you need any help?'

'No, I'm done. I'm just looking at this for fun.'

She looked down at the page and up at me. 'You like maths, huh?'

'Yep, it's my favourite.'

'Why do you like it?'

'It's really . . . neat. When you work something out, then it's finished, and you can always work everything out as long as you know the right way. There's always a definite answer.'

'And everything fits into place?' Suvi asked.

'Yes! Exactly. I like everything to have a place.'

'Me too.' She slid her file neatly back on the shelf.

The front door banged open and Chloe rushed

in, followed by the others. She gave me half a carton of popcorn. 'I saved you some!' she said. 'But you have to take it quick before I eat any more. I was going to save you the whole thing, but then it was just sitting there on my lap and it smelt really good . . . Can I just have one last piece?'

I held out the carton to her, then took a handful myself.

'How was the film?' Suvi asked.

'Saccharine nonsense full of worthy morals for good citizens,' Amelia said.

'She means it had a happy ending,' Chloe said. 'Which was mushy, but the car chases were good.'

'The crashes were the best bit,' Lucy said.

'Was this a suitable film for Lucy?' Suvi asked Dad.

Dad smiled. 'It was one of those CGI animation things.'

'They're the worst,' Suvi said.

Lucy's eyes widened. 'Don't you like anything? What things do you actually like?'

'Maths,' Suvi said in her unexcited voice, but her eyes were smiley at me.

'Say goodnight, Lucy,' Dad said. 'It's past your bedtime.'

'Just a minute, I have to do something.' She

went up to Kirsti's basket and leant over to whisper something to her. She looked like the wicked fairy putting a curse on Sleeping Beauty. Then she turned and clumped up the stairs.

I'm not sure that Lucy likes Kirsti.

CHAPTER ❤ EIGHT

The rest of my first week at St Mark's was OK. I liked the lessons and most of the teachers. I tried to speak up in classes and not to look like a goldfish. Ashandra and Kayleigh seemed to get on all right, but not brilliantly. I remembered what Mum said about people adjusting and what Suvi said about Mum being smart. Maybe it would take a few more weeks before we were completely best friends forever.

It was Dad's turn to have us for the weekend, but he arranged for us to stay at home instead because Suvi's parents were coming from Finland to meet baby Kirsti. I wondered if there would be lots of relations coming to see the baby and if that meant we would miss lots of weekends with Dad, but Mum said that she would take us to the beach all day Saturday so that was a bright side.

Lucy wasn't interested in the beach; she was just cross about not seeing Dad.

'What are they for me?' she asked Amelia on Friday night when we were watching TV.

'What are who for you?' Amelia said, without taking her eyes off the screen.

'Suvi's mum and dad. They're Kirsti's nana and grampy, aren't they? So what are they for me?'

'Two old Finnish people.'

'She means they're not anything for you. You're not related to them,' Chloe said.

'Why not? How come Kirsti gets everyone?'

'You've got people in your family,' I said. 'Like us lot.'

'Kirsti has us lot too.'

'Here, I'll show you, Lucy,' I said. I found a pen and an old envelope on the coffee table and I drew out Lucy's family tree for her. 'See, here's you and here's Kirsti. I used a dotted line because she's your half-sister. And here's Suvi. I did a dotted line for her too because she's your stepmum not your real mum.'

'She's not our stepmum,' Amelia said. 'She's not married to Dad.'

I ignored her. 'And the straight lines are your sisters and the wiggly lines are for grandparents.' I was pleased with the diagram; it made everything neat and clear. I liked looking at how I fitted in with all the people around me.

'That's stupid,' Lucy said, snatching the envelope from me.

'But it makes it easy to understand. You can see exactly what the relationship is between people.'

'What's a relationship?'

'The connection between you and another person. How close you are to someone.'

Lucy shook her head. 'I don't get how I feel from a map. I just feel it.'

But I noticed that she didn't let go of the envelope and her eyes kept running along the dotted line between her and Kirsti.

We had a brilliant time at the beach with Mum (apart from Chloe whacking Amelia round the head with a deckchair and Amelia calling Chloe a cow, but after that they didn't speak to each other so it was more peaceful). We didn't get home until really late so I slept in on Sunday. When I came down into the kitchen, Amelia and Lucy were already there, eating toast and reading. Amelia was hunched over one of those books that has a painting of a lady on the outside and lots of long words on the inside and Lucy was flicking through a catalogue of tools. She'd circled lots of things on the hammer page.

'Where's Mum?' I asked.

'She's asleep in the sitting room,' Amelia said.

'She fell asleep writing lesson plans and drinking coffee,' Lucy added.

'Did you put a blanket over her?' I asked.

Lucy shook her head. 'No, but I did drink her coffee.'

'You're not supposed to drink coffee,' Amelia said. 'Remember that time Dad gave you an espresso and you tried to ride your bike down the library steps?'

'That wasn't because I had coffee; that was because I was training to be a stunt girl.'

I went and put my duvet over Mum.

While I was pouring cornflakes, Chloe came into the kitchen with her new friend, Thunder. I'd seen him at school. He looked large from across the cafeteria, but he looked really large in our kitchen, trying not to knock anything off the counter with his big bottom.

'This is Thunder,' Chloe told us.

'Why are you called Thunder?' Lucy asked.

'Because you can hear him coming from miles away,' Chloe said.

Thunder didn't say anything. He just looked

from Chloe to Lucy to me to Amelia and back to Chloe. 'How many of them are your sisters?' he asked.

'All of them,' Chloe said.

'Wow. You've got a lot. When that new one at your dad's house gets bigger, you'll have enough for a five-a-side team.'

Chloe looked at us again. 'They'd need a lot of work.'

'I'd need a lobotomy before I'd play football,' Amelia said.

'That's when they chop your brain out,' Lucy explained to Thunder.

'Sport is for people who can't read,' Amelia said and she picked up her grown-up book and flounced out.

'Sport is for people who aren't noodle-armed sofa-monkeys!' Chloe called after her.

'If you haven't got a really sharp knife to chop out the brain,' Lucy said to Thunder, 'you can do what the Egyptians did and pull it out through the nose with a hook.'

'Thanks,' Thunder said as if she'd actually given him a useful tip.

I peered into the giant carrier bag Thunder had with him. There was a bear's head in it.

'What's that?' I asked.

'Bear suit,' Thunder said, like that was perfectly normal.

'What for?'

Chloe got a piece of paper out of her back pocket and unfolded it to show us. 'It's a project,' she said.

There were a lot of little cartoon bears on the paper, all of them doing different things.

'We're going to be famous,' Thunder said. 'We're going to film Big Bear in loads of crazy situations and when it goes viral we'll be millionaires.'

'How?' Lucy asked.

'Because everyone will want to watch it.'

'But how will that make you money?'

Thunder's face fell. I'm not sure he'd really thought things through.

Chloe gave him a reassuring punch on the arm. 'We'll sell T-shirts, won't we, Thunder? And mugs and key rings.'

Thunder beamed.

Lucy went off to add a crochet hook to the list of things she wants and Chloe unlocked the back door.

I sat down to eat my cornflakes. 'What are you doing, Clo?'

'We're going to dig up worms.'

'For the bear video?'

'No, this is a different project. We're going to feed them to Buttercup, except we're going to change her name. What do you think of Attila the Bun?'

I didn't like it. 'Mmm.'

Chloe looked at me. 'We can always just keep her as Buttercup.'

'I don't think she'll eat them,' I said. 'Rabbits don't eat worms.'

'This one will,' Thunder said. 'We're going to turn her into a meat eater.'

'It's the first step to creating a vampire bunny,' Chloe explained as they walked out into the garden.

Our garden is much bigger than you'd expect it to be by looking at the front of the house. It's narrow, but the overgrown lawn slopes a long way back to a group of trees that we call the forest. Near the house is Buttercup's hutch and a shed which is jammed full of old scooters and buckets and spades and pots with dried-up plants in. Chloe rummaged around in there until she found a trowel.

While I ate my cereal, I watched them chatting and wiggling worms in front of Buttercup. They laughed a lot. Half the time I didn't even know what they were laughing about, but I could tell they were both having fun.

Lucy came back into the kitchen and rifled through the cupboard under the sink. She pulled out some jam jars and a stack of old newspapers.

'I need some paint,' she said.

'What sort of paint?'

'The white sort.'

'I meant, what do you want to paint? Is it a picture or are you making something?'

'It's secret.'

Lucy says that a lot. She doesn't tell you anything unless she has to. 'I've got a set of watercolours that I got two birthdays ago,' I suggested.

'Is that those titchy little squares? That look like sweets?'

'Yep, except there's no pink because Chloe ate it to see if it tasted like sweets too.'

'Did it?'

'No.' I rinsed out my cereal bowl. 'But it did make her sick pink.'

'I don't want those ones. They're too small. I need lots. Like when you get those buckets of paint.'

'I think there are some tins on the shelf in the shed.'

I glanced out of the window again. Thunder was rolling around on the grass and I could hear Chloe shouting, 'Who's the worm master now?'

'Can you get them down for me?' Lucy asked, opening the back door.

'No way.'

'Why not?'

When Lucy gets into trouble, anyone who saw what she was doing and didn't stop her gets into trouble too. Mum says she's only seven and we have to take care of her. It's a bit like getting a baby crocodile to behave. Except even more bitey.

'I've got to look the other way in case you're doing something Mum ends up saying you shouldn't have,' I said.

Lucy huffed, but she knows the rules.

I turned my back and studied the calendar carefully. It was still on June.

There was some banging from the shed and then I heard Lucy walking back across the kitchen.

'Lucy? You're not going to paint anything really bad, are you?' I said, keeping my back to her.

'Of course not.' She bumped me as she went past. 'I'm going to paint something really good.'

When they'd finished poking worms at Buttercup, Chloe and Thunder went to meet some more of their friends to go bowling and Amelia was shut in her room, so I went to find Lucy. She was in the Pit with something heavy in front of the door.

'Go away!' she said. So I did.

I was pretty bored with no one to hang around with so, as a last resort, I decided to do some homework. Mum woke up and helped me learn my French vocabulary. Then, while she was making Lucy's costume for her Harvest Festival performance, I worked on my chemistry homework. Chemistry is definitely one of my biggest bright sides at school. It's nearly as cool as maths. After I'd finished, I copied out the periodic table so I could stick it next to my bed and learn all the symbols.

When Chloe came home from bowling, I packed up my coloured pencils and went to talk to her.

'Can I ask you something?'

She flopped down on the sofa. 'Yes, but don't sit next to me. I'm very sweaty. Thunder wanted some shots of Big Bear bowling, but that suit is really hot. It is quite good though; little kids think you're a teddy bear.' She fanned herself with one of Mum's magazines. 'Except the ones that think you're going to eat them. Either way, they all scream their heads off.'

'What did Buttercup think of the worms?'

'She's not keen. Thunder thinks we should try them wrapped in lettuce.'

'You're good friends with Thunder, aren't you?'

She yanked off her trainers. 'Yep, he's an idiot.'

'You've got lots of friends.'

'Yeah, loads.'

'Do your friends all get on together?'

'Well, Thunder is always stamping on people, but in a nice way. Most of the time everyone gets on and we have a good laugh.'

'How do you do it? How do you get people to have fun together?'

She peeled off her sweaty socks. 'I suppose we do stuff.'

'Does that make people get along?'

She creased up her forehead. 'I think so. If you go kayaking with someone and then you nearly drown and then you don't drown, it makes you quite friendly.'

That sort of made sense. I suppose if you're trying not to fall into a raging river then you wouldn't have time for arguing.

'But we don't do kayaking at school,' I said.

'Kayaking is best, but you could do rugby or join the swimming team or anything where you're all doing it together.'

I'm not crazy about sport like Chloe is, but I thought it was a good idea. Being super nice didn't seem to be helping Ashandra and Kayleigh become

81

best friends so maybe I needed to get them to join a team with me, then they could see how much fun we could all have together.

Later on, Mum managed to persuade Lucy to come out of the Pit and Chloe to stop playing computer games. She couldn't make Amelia come out of her room, but the rest of us had a biscuit-making competition without her; Chloe and Lucy against me and Mum. Chloe pretended to like her and Lucy's banana and chilli cookies, but Mum's and my chocolate chip ones were nicer. Mum agreed; she gave me a big high five when we did the tasting.

Chloe was right; it does feel good to be part of a team.

CHAPTER ❤ NINE

'I thought you were right off PE,' Kayleigh said on Monday morning when I asked her about joining a team.

'I'm just off basketball.'

She pushed an escaping strand of hair behind her ear. 'Well, I've always wanted to play polo.'

'The one on horses or the one in a swimming pool?'

'On horses of course.'

'I'm not sure our school has got a team for that.'

In the end, we decided to take a look at the sports noticeboard before registration. There were a lot of teams, but most of them seemed to be already filled and the notices were about practices or matches. They were looking for more people for gymnastics, but you had to do a try-out for that. I can't even do a cartwheel so I didn't think I had a very good chance of getting chosen.

Then I saw a poster for Year Seven Hockey Club, which said 'everyone welcome'. When they write that, it means that you can come even if you're rubbish because they don't have enough people to be fussy about it. They'd even underlined the 'everyone', that's how not fussy they were.

'That sounds good,' Kayleigh said.

'Ash will be good at that,' I said. 'She's a fast runner.'

'You're going to ask Ashandra too?'

'I think she'll like hockey, don't you?'

Kayleigh's face looked like she didn't care at all whether Ashandra would be good at hockey, which was disappointing, but she managed to say, 'I suppose.'

But, when we got to registration and I asked her, Ashandra didn't seem sure either.

'I already go to karate and choir; even someone as brilliant as me needs to sleep now and again.'

She was joking, but Kayleigh pulled a face.

'And I need to make sure I've got enough time to do homework.'

'It's at lunchtime; it won't interfere with your homework,' I promised.

'What about when there are matches?'

Kayleigh pursed her lips. 'What makes you think you'd get on the team?'

'I normally get into teams.'

Ash was only telling the truth, but I supposed that if you don't know someone well enough to know that they've been on lots of teams then you might think they're being a big-headed boaster. And that might make you mouth 'show off'.

'Please join,' I said quickly before Kayleigh could say anything out loud. 'Just try it for a few weeks.'

Ashandra let out her breath. 'Oh, all right.'

'Brilliant, I'll put our names down at breaktime.'

They didn't look very brilliantish about it, but once we started playing together I knew it would help them get on.

When Miss Espinoza arrived, I went to my own desk. The tight plait girl, who I now knew was called Alenka, looked up when I sat next to her and then down again.

'Hi,' I said. 'Did you have a nice weekend?'

She thought about it. 'Some of it was nice. My sister, she took me out for a milkshake.'

'Wow. My big sister would never do that. I mean, if she took me, she would have to take my other sisters and Chloe can drink a lot of milkshake. It would cost loads.'

'My sister is in Year Nine. She's really nice. When I have a bad day, she always takes me for a milkshake.'

She didn't say why she'd needed cheering up.

'Me and Ash and Kayleigh are going to do hockey on Thursday lunchtimes. Do you want to come too?'

I thought she was going to say no. I think she thought she was going to say no too because when she said, 'OK,' she seemed as surprised as I was.

We had chips from the chip shop for tea. I love chips, but the smell of them always makes me a bit worried. When it's beans on toast for tea, that means Mum has had a bad day and is very tired, but chips mean a terrible day. So terrible that Mum doesn't even have the energy to open a tin of beans.

'Are you OK?' I asked her. I was clearing up the chip papers, Lucy was pretending to help and Mum was surrounded by her class's writing journals.

'I'm fine, Ella. I've just got a lot of marking to do.'

'Again?' Lucy asked. 'You did marking last week.'

Actually, Mum didn't do very much marking last week because she spent so much time on Lucy's Harvest Festival costume and making sure she knew her lines.

Mum looked down at the journals. 'I'm afraid there's marking every week. It just keeps coming! Every day the little horrors produce more writing. Even the really fidgety ones squeeze out a few lines that I'm supposed to read and comment on. The head expects me to have written something on every single piece of writing.'

'So why haven't you?' Lucy asked.

'Because there are thirty children in my class and they do a piece of writing every single day. Even if I only spend five minutes marking each piece that's still two and a half hours of marking.'

Lucy put her head on one side. 'You could do that. You could do it when I'm in bed and I don't need you.'

When Lucy is in bed, Mum does the washing and makes packed lunches and helps me and Chloe with our homework and listens to Amelia talking about how unreasonable her science teacher is.

Mum sighed. 'There just don't seem to be enough hours in the day.'

'Maybe you should sleep less,' Lucy said. I don't think she's noticed the dark circles under Mum's eyes.

'You could stop ironing,' I said. 'Chloe just crumples everything anyway.'

Mum smiled that smile that grown-ups do when

they think you're sweet, but you don't understand enough to do anything really useful.

I really wanted to understand. I really wanted to do something useful. After all, if I was trying to be nice to everyone then my mum deserved it most of all.

'I could make beans on toast tomorrow,' I said.

'Thank you, Ella. I would appreciate that. And I think I'll need you girls to help a little around the house generally this term.'

Lucy threw a scrunched-up ball of chip paper at the bin and missed. 'We already do the washing-up and the hoovering. If we do anything else, you'll have to pay us.'

Mum laughed. 'All right, you do some cooking and cleaning and I'll pay you with food and shelter and the endless love of a mother. How does that sound?'

'Sounds like you can't buy sweets with it like you do with real money,' she said and stomped off to the Pit again.

I finished tidying up and, when I looked at Mum, she was still frowning at her books.

'Don't worry too much,' I said. 'I don't think everybody reads all the corrections that teachers put. If they did, Lucy would be able to spell "assassinate" properly by now.'

Mum pushed her hair out of her eyes. 'But I have to set targets. The trouble is, lots of them need to work on the same area so I'm writing the same thing over and over.'

'Maybe I could write some for you?'

'I don't think that's allowed.'

I had an idea. 'I could make you some stickers!'

So I got on the computer and typed out Mum's most used comments. First, I did smiley faces that tell you what you're doing right (*Sparkling vocabulary! Excellent use of capital letters! Nice connectives!*). And then I typed out what you need to improve to get to the next level. (*Use full stops! Check your spelling! How about some wow words?*). I printed them on address labels and Mum just stuck the appropriate ones in the books. Even then, she couldn't resist adding a personal comment occasionally, but it made things much quicker.

'Thank you, Ella,' Mum said. 'You've been extremely helpful.'

I was really glad I could help Mum feel less stressed. I just wished I could sort out Ashandra and Kayleigh as easily.

CHAPTER ✦ TEN

Wednesday night at Dad's wasn't fun. Dad told Lucy to stop sticking her head in Kirsti's basket. Lucy shouted at Dad and then had a go at Suvi too. For once, even Suvi looked like she was about to lose her temper; she took Kirsti upstairs for her bath, even though it wasn't time. Somehow, Amelia managed to join in by shouting at Dad and Chloe, and then at me when I asked her if she was all right.

In the morning, after Dad woke us up, Amelia went back to sleep. When I'd finished breakfast, she was only just staggering downstairs, even though we needed to leave really soon.

'Why didn't you wake me again?' she asked Suvi.

'You knew it was school today, yes?' Suvi asked.

'Of course I knew it was school! I'm not an imbecile.'

'Then you know you have to get up.'

Amelia picked up her bag and walked straight out of the door, slamming it behind her.

'She didn't have any cereal! Not even as a Magic Breakfast!' Chloe said to me.

That wasn't really the bit that shocked me most. I dragged Chloe into the upstairs bathroom and locked the door behind us. It's the only place at Dad's house that you can have a private conversation.

'Is this about panda-eyes, pig-face Amelia?' Chloe asked.

I shook my head. I didn't see what we could possibly do about Amelia and her stomping.

'Did you see what Lucy was doing at the table?' I asked Chloe.

'No. I was checking how much Weetabix I can store in my cheeks.'

I stared at her.

'You know, like a hamster? I got a whole one in, but that wouldn't last you, would it? Mine's nearly all gone already.' She opened her mouth to show me some Weetabixy slop that was still between her teeth and her cheek.

'It looks like your teeth are rotting.'

Chloe looked in the mirror and bared her teeth. There were brown speckles all over them. 'Cool.' She grinned at me. 'What did Lucy do at breakfast?'

'She glared.'

'What at?'

'Kirsti. The whole time. I don't think she likes her.'

'Does Lucy like anyone?'

'Yes!'

People think that, because Lucy is always stamping her feet and telling everyone how big their bottom is, she doesn't like anyone, but actually she cares about people a lot. She just does it in quite a fierce way.

'Lucy loves us. Remember that time she fell out of a tree because she was trying to get your ball back? And, even though she says Amelia smells, when Kayleigh said Amelia was moody, Lucy kicked her in the shins.'

'So how can you tell whether she likes Kirsti or not?'

'With all of us, she either says rude things or she squishes us in killer hugs, but with Kirsti she just keeps staring at her like she's thinking.'

When Lucy is thinking, it usually means trouble.

I rubbed my hand over my face. 'What if she wants to get rid of her?'

Chloe dabbed at her teeth with Dad's toothbrush. 'What do you mean?'

'Remember that time she tried to sell Buttercup to the postman?'

'Buttercup isn't a baby.'

'No, but we never had a baby before. I don't know what she'll try and do.'

Chloe looked thoughtful for a moment and then nodded. 'We'd better keep an eye on her.'

Downstairs, Dad was calmly drinking a cup of coffee and Suvi was breastfeeding Kirsti. It was much quieter at Dad's house than mornings at home. Lucy was drinking a glass of milk and looking at Dad and Suvi's bookshelf. It's probably the most colourful thing in the room, even though the book spines have got very boring titles about sustainability and environmental impact and management in education.

'There's nothing to read here!' Lucy announced.

Suvi detached Kirsti from her chest and put her down on her mat. 'All these books and papers are a bit grown up for you,' she said to Lucy. 'Maybe you can bring a picture book from home.'

'I'm too old for picture books! I know how to read,' Lucy said and she picked up a newspaper from the table and sat down next to Kirsti. She opened out the newspaper, blocking everyone's view of the baby.

I looked at Chloe.

'She can't do anything to her now,' Chloe whispered. 'There are too many people in the room.'

But I remembered the time Lucy managed to eat a whole Easter egg without anyone noticing, even though we were all playing Monopoly together.

It was my Easter egg.

I kept my eye on her.

She was muttering to herself, but I couldn't tell if she was reading the paper or being mean to the baby. I guessed Kirsti wouldn't understand anyway.

'We'd better get going.' Dad drained his coffee. 'What's going on in world affairs?' he asked Lucy.

Lucy lowered the paper. 'Somebody shot somebody.'

'Oh.'

'They should put more shooting in children's books. Children would get better at reading more quicker if they could read about the blood.'

Dad reached out and took away the paper. 'Time for school.'

Lucy scowled. 'I'll be back,' she said in a low growl to Kirsti.

'See?' I whispered to Chloe. 'That didn't look very friendly, did it?'

'She always screws up her face like that. She had the exact same face when we brought in her birthday cake last year.'

We got our things and headed off for school. I called for Ashandra and she told me a funny story about her brother's friend skateboarding down the corridor and straight into Mr O'Brien, but all I could think about was why couldn't Lucy get on with Kirsti? Why couldn't Chloe not call Amelia names? Why couldn't Amelia not hate so many people? And why couldn't Mum and Dad stand to be in the same room as each other?

I wished everyone would just get on with everyone else.

CHAPTER ❧ ELEVEN

Art is not my favourite subject. Kayleigh says that if you're going to be creative then it's good to have loads of art materials spread all around you, but I don't like how messy the art room always is. My worst thing is when Miss Gardner says, 'Free choice today. Go mad, use your imagination!' because I never know what to do. I prefer it when she says, 'Sketch a pencil portrait of your partner.' Even then I like to ask her how big it should be and whether we're allowed to do rubbing out.

So I was quite happy when Miss Gardner announced that we were going to be in an art competition. Competitions have rules.

'As you know, we've got International Day coming up next month,' she said. 'Each of the Year

Seven and Year Eight tutor groups will be given one of these . . .' She pointed to a large canvas panel on a frame. 'You'll be assigned a country and your job is to represent that country on your panel. They'll be displayed on International Day so your parents will have the opportunity to see them and the best one will win a prize.'

That all seemed clear, but then she said, 'This is a class project so I want you to do everything yourselves.'

I wasn't sure if we'd be able to get a panel done if she left us to it. I didn't know if our class could organise themselves.

'But who will be in charge?' I asked.

'I think perhaps it would best if we choose a couple of people to coordinate, just so that everybody knows what they're doing. Who thinks they could do a good job of managing things?'

Jasmine put her hand up before Miss Gardner had even finished the question. I'm not sure it's very smart for teachers to ask questions like that because often the people who think they're good at managing are the people who just like bossing everyone about. Eight other people put up their hands, including Ashandra and Kayleigh. I didn't.

Miss Gardner looked the volunteers over. 'I think we'll have Ashandra and Kayleigh,' she said.

Jasmine sucked in her breath and pinched up her face.

Nobody else was surprised. We'd been at school for less than three weeks, but everybody knew that Ashandra is the smart, confident girl that teachers always pick for stuff. And we'd all sighed with envy looking at Kayleigh's paintings and drawings so it was obvious she was a good choice for an art project.

Jasmine pays more attention to what she wants than what's obvious so she kept on scowling.

Miss Gardner let Alenka pull a slip of paper out of a bag. We got China. Miss Gardner said that today was for finishing off our jungle scenes, but next lesson Ashandra and Kayleigh would take over and we'd get to work on bringing the spirit of China to our panel.

I was so excited thinking about Ashandra and Kayleigh working together that I almost forgot that it was our first Hockey Club at lunchtime. Luckily, everybody else remembered. I was pleased that I had asked Alenka, mostly because she was really keen, but also because she seemed a tiny bit nervous like me. Ashandra and Kayleigh, on the other hand, were acting completely normal and didn't seem to be worrying about a hockey stick slipping out of their sweaty hands at all. We got changed and headed out on to the field.

The thing that I've discovered about sport is that it's not just how good you are that matters; it's how good people expect you to be. Chloe's got powerful legs and a sturdy body: people expect her to be good at sport and she is. But Lucy, who's tiny with copper curls, looks like the kind of china doll that you're afraid to pick up in case you break it so no one expects her to be an athlete. On sports day, everyone smiles when she lines up for a race. She never actually wins, but she looks so little, and like she's trying so hard, that she always gets a cheer when she crosses the finishing line.

My issue is my height. If you're tall, people expect two things from you: being mature and being good at sport. I'm actually not that bad at PE. I can run fast-ish and I can catch and throw reasonably well. You have to be able to catch in our house because people are always throwing things and if you don't react quickly enough you'll end up with a face full of stinky socks or Lucy's toast crusts. The problem I have with sport is not that I'm middle-ish at it: it's that people expect me to be brilliant. And when you're expecting something amazing anything else just looks rubbish. So, even though hockey was my idea, I was really nervous about people being disappointed in me.

Luckily, none of the thirty-two girls who turned

up for Hockey Club had played any hockey before and we were all rubbish. Which was really nice. The club was run by a different teacher to the one we have for PE lessons and she didn't say, 'You ought to be good at this,' or 'Use those long legs,' or any of the stuff I usually get shouted at me.

The only downside was that Jasmine and her friends, Asia and Courtney, were there. Every time Mrs Henderson got us to line up, I stood as far away from them as possible.

First, we learnt how to hold the stick and then we practised getting the ball to stop, which was more difficult than you'd think. When we got to dribbling the ball round cones, it was complete chaos: there were balls everywhere.

'Watch it! That's mine!' Jasmine snapped when I went after what I thought was my ball. 'Why are you even here?' she asked. 'You'll just get your long legs tied in a knot.'

I kept my head down and picked up a different ball. Why was she so horrible? I almost wished I hadn't bothered coming and that I was sitting in the cafeteria, eating a ham sandwich, but then I saw Kayleigh giggling at Ashandra pretending to play her stick like a guitar and I knew it was all worthwhile.

*

When Lucy came in with Mum that evening, she poked me in the middle.

'Can you watch me be a bat?' she asked.

Lucy likes pretending to be a bat. She hangs upside down by her knees from a climbing frame at the skatepark down the road and thinks battish things. But she isn't allowed to go to the park by herself.

I was in the middle of my homework, but Lucy looked a bit droopy so I said yes. When we got there, a boy a bit younger than me was on the skate ramp, but no one else. I was glad; sometimes when we go to the park there are loads of older boys and I feel a bit embarrassed. Especially when they stare at Lucy while she's being a bat. Lucy scrambled up the climbing frame and swung into position. She let out a sigh like she'd just leant back in a really comfy armchair.

I balanced on the bottom rung of the frame.

'What do you think Kirsti is doing now?' Lucy asked.

'I'm pretty sure she's either feeding or sleeping.'

'Or gurgling. Sometimes she makes noises like Chloe's stomach does after she's eaten curry.'

I thought that if Lucy was feeling really relaxed and bat-like it might be a good time to ask her about Kirsti.

101

'Lucy? Why are you always thinking about Kirsti? Are you sad that you're not the baby any more?'

Lucy turned her head to look at me. 'Why would I want to be a baby?'

'You *were* the baby until Kirsti was born.'

Lucy's eyes sparked up like flames. 'I was not! I haven't been a baby for years and years. Who wants to be a baby? You have to wear stupid hats and eat sloppy things.'

'So why are you so . . . interested in Kirsti?'

'She's my sister,' she said, looking at me like I was mad.

'But why are you always hanging around her when we're at Dad's? And why do you keep staring at her?'

Lucy wrinkled her nose. 'I told you, she's my sister.'

And then I understood that Lucy hadn't been acting mean to Kirsti, or at least not any meaner than she is to anyone else; she was just spending time with her.

'I know Kirsti's your sister,' I said, 'but Amelia's your sister too and you don't spend ages talking to her.'

'I could if I wanted to.'

'But you don't.'

'But I *could*. Because she's near me. Amelia, Chloe and you are all my sisters so you're in my house. All the time.'

'And that's a good thing?'

'That's what it's supposed to be. All your family should be in your house.'

I felt a bit sad because, even though Lucy didn't want to be the baby, she was still little and I didn't think she completely understood divorce. 'I know some families are like that,' I said. 'But when parents split up people live in different houses.'

'Mum and Dad could buy one big house and we could all live in that.'

I sighed. 'I don't think that will happen.'

'Why not?'

'Because Mum and Dad don't love each other any more.'

Lucy huffed. 'They don't have to do love stuff to be in the same house!' She started swinging backwards and forwards. Her face was pink and angry. 'I don't want Kirsti to be ruined. She's supposed to be a Strawberry Sister like us, but she doesn't know anything. She doesn't know about burping competitions, or licking a cake to bagsie it, and she's never even played March of the Zombies.'

'She's a bit small for March of the Zombies.'

Lucy shook her head at me like I was an idiot. 'What do you think will happen to all the babies when the zombies come? You're never too young to be a zombie.'

'We'll see Kirsti whenever we go to Dad's,' I said.

Lucy put her hands on the bar beneath her, then flipped her legs over so she landed on the ground.

'It's not the same as having her in our house.' Her face was all scrunched up.

I was getting really hungry and cold, but I wanted to be nice so I tried to think of a way to make Lucy feel better.

'You could help Kirsti be a Strawberry Sister,' I suggested.

'Could I?'

'Yep, you could be in charge.' Lucy likes being in charge. 'You could make sure that she knows all our family things. Teach her our games and take her to our special places. Show her what it means to be a Strawberry Sister.'

Lucy was still frowning, but I could tell she was thinking about it.

When we got back from the park, I went looking for Chloe. I found her feeding Buttercup. Luckily for Buttercup, it looked like she was getting a vegetarian dinner this time.

'Lucy doesn't hate Kirsti,' I said.

'That's good,' Chloe said, nibbling on a bit of Buttercup's lettuce.

'She's upset that Kirsti doesn't live with us. She actually really loves her.'

'That's good too,' she said. 'You have to love your family. Except for complete traitors called Amelia. You have to spit at those ones.' She scowled up at Amelia's window. 'It's good about Lucy.'

I thought about that later when I was in bed. Because Chloe was right: it *was* good that Lucy loved Kirsti. Having a family to love is definitely a bright side. But somehow it was still a problem. It was making Lucy unhappy. But I knew that the answer wasn't for Lucy to love Kirsti any less.

When you're little, you think that love is a really good answer to all your problems. It's what makes you feel better when you fall over and your mum cuddles you, and the thing that makes you feel safe at night when your dad tucks you in; it's the happy storybook ending where the prince and princess get married or the characters become friends forever.

But maybe love isn't always the answer. Maybe sometimes how much you love someone leads to questions too. Hard questions.

CHAPTER 🍓 TWELVE

Saturdays at home are quite pyjama-y. Chloe usually goes out to do something sporty with her friends and the rest of us stay at home and watch TV and read books and chat to Mum and eat lots of sandwiches.

It's not like that at Dad's house. At Dad's house, there's always a Plan. It's not always the same thing because my dad changes what he's into all the time. It used to drive my mum mad, especially when he'd come home with a new gadget or even more sports equipment. Sometimes I like my dad's new hobbies and sometimes I don't. Last year he got really into geocaching and we used to hike round the countryside, using a GPS device to look for secret boxes. I liked finding the coordinates and Chloe liked racing about on the moors, but Lucy got bored and Amelia wouldn't join in. After a while, Dad didn't seem so keen.

Then he got a pottery wheel. I didn't like that. Clay is really messy and it never does what you want it to.

Then it was cycling. I quite liked that, except when we went riding in the woods and the paths were really bumpy and I nearly went crashing into a bush. We still go cycling sometimes, but today's Plan was fishing.

Dad got everyone up very early, except for Suvi and Kirsti who he said were having a lie-in because Kirsti had been awake for half the night. 'I've got a lot of work to do this afternoon,' Dad said. 'So I want to get an early start.'

Lucy hadn't been awake half the night, but she was still quite grumpy.

'Fishing for fish?' she asked.

'Of course for fish,' Dad said, whipping away her breakfast plate.

Lucy narrowed her eyes. 'Sometimes in cartoons when they go fishing they pull out a boot or a tyre on the end of their hook.'

'I think the general idea is to avoid rubbish and stick to fish.'

'I'd like a tyre better than a fish. You can make a swing out of a tyre.'

Dad took some water bottles out of the fridge and put them in a bag. 'OK, Lucy, you fish for junk and the rest of us will try to catch our supper.'

Lucy shook her head. 'I can't fish anyway. I've got ballet.'

Dad said something rude about ballet. Even though Lucy goes every Saturday, Dad is always forgetting about it.

'It's teaching me to be graceful.' Lucy flopped across the table with her legs in the air to steal a slice of Chloe's toast. 'Anyway, I want to try to saw Madame Donna in half.'

'Does Madame Donna like it when you do magic tricks on her?' Chloe asked.

'I don't always tell her exactly what the trick is.'

Dad looked at Lucy for a few seconds, then turned to Chloe. 'You're looking forward to fishing, aren't you, Chloe?'

'Yep, I'm going to be brilliant at it. And, while we're doing it, you can help me with my Fantasy Football team.'

Dad beamed. 'Excellent.'

Amelia made a vomiting noise. Dad turned to where she was slumped on the sofa.

'There's no need for that. You know, it's nice and quiet by the river; you could sing us one of your songs.'

Amelia lifted her head. 'Or I could stay in bed like normal people do at the crack of dawn on a Saturday. Anyway, since when have you been interested in my singing?' And then she slumped back down face first.

'Amelia hasn't got time for us,' Chloe said. 'She needs hours to put on all her make-up and then she's got to text all her friends about whether some idiot boy looked at her or not.'

But Dad was still trying to get someone other than Chloe excited about fishing.

'There'll be maggots, Lucy! You like wriggly, squirmy things, don't you?'

'Yeah, that's why she likes you, Dad,' Amelia said and she rolled off the sofa and crawled back upstairs.

'That was quite rude,' Chloe said. 'You ought to speak to her about her attitude, Dad.'

Dad blinked. Chloe doesn't normally talk in that teacherish way.

'I'll come,' I said. I wasn't exactly keen on fishing, but it would be nice to spend some time with Dad and he seemed so excited that I didn't want to disappoint him.

'You're all coming,' he said.

Lucy waved a ballet shoe at him.

'Except Lucy.'

A door closed upstairs.

'And Amelia.'

In the end, we left Amelia in bed and dropped off Lucy at the community centre for her lesson. Then we headed out of town to the neighbouring village, parked the car at a pub and made our way to the river.

'But won't Lucy need picking up soon?' I asked.

'I asked Rose's mum to drop her back at home. We can stay for a few hours.'

Chloe started telling Dad about football transfers. I wasn't sure if they were real ones or fantasy ones. I just hoped that wasn't the only thing they were going to talk about.

It was pretty down by the river. The sun was shining and birds were singing. The trees were leaning over the bank like they were admiring themselves in the water. It was very calm and peaceful.

'I wish we had an air pistol,' Chloe said.

Dad set up a couple of deckchairs and showed Chloe how to bait a line. We only had two rods so I just had to watch. Once the lines were in the water, there wasn't that much to do so they talked some more about football. A lot more.

'Can we talk about something else?' I asked.

So they talked about rugby. And then rally driving.

Eventually, Chloe said, 'Sorry, Ella, I've had ages. It's your turn.' And she gave the rod to me. 'Actually, I saw a kind of burrow hole back there. I'm going to go and see if there are any vicious badgers in it.'

'Don't disappear,' Dad said.

So then I got to copy Dad casting his line. He got tangled up the first time so I'm not sure that he was a really good example to follow, but eventually we both got everything where it was supposed to be. I sat back in my chair. It was nice being outside and having Dad all to myself for once.

But I couldn't think of anything to say.

It was quiet for a minute. Dad yawned.

'Kirsti's nice,' I said eventually.

'She's a bonny baby, isn't she? You know, I was working so hard when you girls were small that I missed out on a lot of things. I'm really looking forward to seeing this little one grow and flourish.'

'You can still watch us growing up too,' I said.

'Yes, yes, of course.'

If I hadn't been being super nice, I might have thought that he seemed to say that in quite a quick way, like he didn't really mean it; instead, I tried to say something else about Kirsti, but I couldn't really think of anything because she didn't exactly do a lot.

There was a long pause.

'How's Mum?' Dad asked.

I didn't know what I was supposed to say to that. Was Mum supposed to be happy or sad without him?

'She's fine.'

'Good.' He leant back in his chair and closed his eyes. 'And how's school?'

I knew the answer to that one. 'It's great because now Ashandra is at the same school as me and Kayleigh so we can all be friends together.' I stared at the water. 'I mean . . . we're not exactly *best*, best friends at the moment. Actually, Kayleigh said something not that nice about Ashandra the other day, and also Ashandra didn't want to work with us on a book project, but we've all joined the Hockey Club so that's good.' I squeezed the fishing rod tight. 'In the end, I think we'll all be really good friends. Don't you?'

I looked at Dad. He was fast asleep.

I didn't wake him up. When Chloe came back, she took the rod gently out of his hands. She said that she heard him walking about with Kirsti in the middle of the night so he must have been tired.

Sometimes it's difficult to think of the bright side of a baby who takes up all your dad's spare time, even when she's not there.

We thought we'd got a bite on the fishing line at one point, but when we managed to reel it in it was only a chunk of wood.

Eventually, Dad woke up and took us home for lunch.

The afternoon's Plan was much smaller because Dad needed to do some work. He said we just had time to take Kirsti for a quick walk round the park before he got started.

'You're not coming, are you?' Amelia asked Suvi while Dad was changing Kirsti.

'I think I will stay here and make some phone calls,' Suvi said, but her face looked like she'd wanted to say something else.

It takes a long time to get out of the house when you've got a baby with you. First you have to make sure that they're not hungry and that their nappy is clean. Then you have to check that they won't be too cold or too hot. Dad had a ginormous bag full of things to take with us, even though we were only going down the road.

'Don't be long,' Suvi said as we were leaving. 'Kirsti will need another feed soon.'

We piled out of the door. Dad stopped to adjust

the handle on Kirsti's pram and an old lady walking past peered in at Kirsti.

'Isn't she lovely?' she said. 'Goodness, are all these girls yours?' she asked Dad.

'Every one.'

She beamed at us. 'How splendid. You must be very proud. Five little treasures.'

Dad smiled back. 'Sometimes it's more like five little monkeys!' He put his arm round Lucy. 'They're good girls really. You make your old dad proud, don't you?'

I didn't know that I made Dad proud, but I smiled at the old lady. Amelia cracked her chewing gum.

'Enjoy the weather while it lasts,' the old lady said and she was off.

'Who was that?' Lucy asked.

'I don't know,' Dad said. 'A nice lady.'

'Why was she talking about us?'

'I think she was impressed that I've managed to produce such a handsome, well-behaved brood.'

Kirsti let out a wail, Chloe burped and Amelia said a bad word.

'I think she thought we were famous,' Lucy said.

The walk didn't last long. Kirsti cried a lot. Lucy asked a lot of questions about why Kirsti cries so much. Chloe didn't stop talking to Dad and Amelia didn't say a word. I offered to get another blanket out of the bag in case she was cold, but Dad said no. Then I said I could push the pram if he was still tired, but he didn't want me to do that either. It's quite hard being nice when people don't want your help.

When we got back, Dad disappeared into his study and we hardly saw him again that weekend.

CHAPTER ✿ THIRTEEN

I was really pleased when Ashandra said she wanted to sit with me and Kayleigh at lunch on Tuesday, but it turned out that she just wanted to talk about the art competition.

'Do you want to show everyone your research first in class or shall I?' she asked Kayleigh.

'You can show yours,' Kayleigh said. 'Actually, I haven't exactly got very much research.'

Ashandra pursed her lips. 'Why not? We agreed on Friday that we'd get our research done this weekend. You heard us talking about it, didn't you, Ella?'

To be fair, it was mostly Ashandra that I'd heard talking about it. Although Kayleigh definitely did do some head-nodding. Before I was forced to answer, Kay folded her arms. 'I don't really think we need to do all this research stuff; we should get on with decorating our panel.'

'We need to know what we're going to put on it first.'

'I've got loads of ideas.'

'Yeah, but it's not going to be a very accurate representation of Chinese culture if we don't have a solid foundation of research.'

When big words come out of Ashandra's mouth, they seem to clog up Kayleigh's ears and she doesn't listen to anything else. She rolled her eyes at me.

'Kayleigh?' Ashandra tapped the table. 'We're supposed to be in charge of the project.'

'Seems like you're being in charge enough for both of us.'

'Somebody has to be responsible and not act like a little kid.'

Kayleigh clenched her jaw. 'Are you calling me a baby?'

Ashandra drew herself up tall. 'I'm saying that you're irresponsible and you're letting the class down.'

'That's better than being a stuck-up bossy-pants who thinks she's better than everyone else.' Kayleigh pushed back her chair and flounced off to the drinks machine.

Ashandra stood up with her head held high and walked off in the opposite direction.

I was left in the middle.

'Has Miss Gardner told your class about the art competition yet?' Chloe asked me while we were making pasta bake for tea. Amelia was supposed to be in charge, but she was scribbling in a notebook.

'Yes,' I said. Ashandra and Kayleigh had ignored each other all day after their row. It made me feel sick just thinking about it.

Chloe was distracted by Amelia noisily leafing through her notebook.

'Amelia, you're supposed to be doing the peppers,' Chloe said.

'I'm doing something more important.'

'Nothing's more important than making food for me to eat.'

'I'm writing a song for International Day. But I wouldn't expect you to understand the importance of music in an otherwise bleak existence.'

'Has it got any rude words in it?' Chloe asked.

Amelia rolled her head back like she couldn't even bear to listen to Chloe. 'No, it has not.'

'Then I don't think it's as important as making tea.'

'We're doing China for our panel,' I interrupted

before full-scale war broke out. 'Did you know they're going to be on display in the hall on International Day when the parents come in the afternoon? Do you think Dad will come?'

'Yes,' Chloe said.

'No,' said Amelia at the same time. 'He didn't bother coming to see me sing my solo in the carol concert.'

Chloe bit into a chocolate finger. I don't know where she got it from. There weren't any in the cupboard. 'You can't really blame Dad for not wanting to listen to you sing,' she said through her biscuit. 'It is super boring.'

Amelia opened her mouth, but I interrupted again. 'What country are your class doing?' I asked Chloe. 'For your panel?'

Chloe looked back at me. 'We've got Finland. I'm going to ask Suvi for ideas.'

Amelia pulled a face. 'What are you asking the Ice Queen for?'

'Because that's where she's from obviously.'

'It's revolting the way you suck up to her and Dad.'

'I don't suck up to them! I'm just not rude and horrible like you are.'

Amelia put down her pencil. 'You just don't get it, do you?'

'Get what?'

'You've got no sense of solidarity with Mum.'

'What on earth are you talking about?'

Amelia gave her a withering look. 'You don't understand anything. You're too immature.'

Chloe slammed the casserole dish down hard on the counter. 'I'm twelve! I can be immature if I want to! Why do people want me to act a certain way and do stupid grown-up stuff? You think you're an adult because you're always being sarcastic and reading boring books and talking about boys. If that's being grown up then I'd rather be immature.'

'That's not what I'm talking about! I'm talking about looking after Mum, but you obviously don't care about that.' Amelia snatched up her notebook. 'You don't care about anything!' She stormed out of the kitchen.

'Yes I do!' shouted Chloe. And she went out into the back garden, throwing open the door so hard that it smacked against the wall.

I was left in the middle.

CHAPTER ❦ FOURTEEN

Kayleigh let Ashandra completely take charge in art on Thursday. And then she didn't bother coming to Hockey Club; she didn't even care when I told her that she'd missed learning how to shoot goals.

I was starting to think that maybe Chloe's suggestion about doing things together wasn't going to be enough. Maybe nothing was going to make them friends. And anyway Chloe wasn't the expert on friendship that I thought she was because for days all she and Amelia had said to each other were horrible things, even though it wasn't that long ago that they were really good mates and shared a bedroom. By Friday night, they were still angry with each other.

'Which one of you snot trails has got my

phone?' Amelia demanded, interrupting me and Chloe arm-wrestling.

'Why would we want your phone?' Chloe stuck out her tongue.

I rubbed my arm and didn't say anything.

'Because my phone is much better than yours.'

Chloe flexed her hand. 'Yeah, but it probably goes around telling all the other phones how it's better than them and so mature. Nobody likes phones like that.'

'You think you're so funny. You're not!'

'Why is Mum laughing then?'

We all turned to look at Mum who was trying to hang up the washing on bits of furniture because it was raining outside. There was definitely a smile on her face.

'I'm not laughing,' she said. 'I'm just enjoying the lively nature of your exchange.' She looked round the sitting room; there were soggy clothes hanging from the radiators and chairs, and the floor was covered with various cups and plates from after-school snacks and bits of magazines that Lucy had made a collage from. 'I haven't seen your phone in here, Amelia, but it could be under any of these school jumpers or piles of junk. Where did you have it last?'

'In my bedroom, which means someone has been in there.'

'Wasn't me,' Chloe said. 'I'm allergic to both

disgusting perfume and whiney music so I can't go in your room without breaking out in a rash.'

Amelia ignored her. 'Where's Lucy?'

'She's at Dad's,' I said.

Lucy had managed to persuade Suvi to pick her up from After School Club sometimes even when it wasn't a Wednesday or a second weekend. She hadn't really told anyone why, but I knew it was because she wanted to see Kirsti.

'No, she's back now,' Mum said. 'Dad dropped her off half an hour ago.'

'She's probably in the Pit,' I said.

Mum frowned. 'She's spending too much time down there.'

'I'll help you look for your phone,' I said to Amelia.

That meant Amelia stayed in the sitting room and carried on moaning to Mum about how we steal her stuff while I looked in the kitchen and the bathroom and on the stairs. I found her sunglasses in the kitchen cupboard and her new boots under a damp towel in the bathroom, but there was no sign of her phone. I was going to look in the Pit too, but there was a big sign taped on the door that said KEEP OUT in Lucy's handwriting. Underneath there was a picture. I'm not sure exactly what it was supposed to be, but it had a lot of teeth.

Eventually, I found Amelia's mobile in the cupboard under the stairs.

Lucy was talking into it.

'Lucy! Amelia is going mad looking for that.'

She ignored me and carried on speaking. '. . . And if you want to make a really big splash you need to get a good run-up—' She paused to flick her wrist at me, meaning I should go away, but I stood firm.

'Who are you talking to?' I asked.

'Kirsti.'

'Kirsti's a baby. She can't talk yet.'

'No, but she can listen. She's a good listener.'

My brain felt a bit like scrambled egg. 'But how did she answer the phone?'

'She didn't answer it. She rang me.'

For a second, I wondered if all that time Lucy was whispering to Kirsti she had been teaching her some incredible baby tricks. 'What?'

'I borrowed Amelia's phone then, when I was at Dad's, I used his cordless phone to ring the mobile and I answered it and then I left the cordless under Kirsti's cot.'

'But you've been back from Dad's for nearly an hour now.'

'So?'

'Has Dad's phone been connected to Amelia's mobile all that time?'

'*Yes*,' Lucy said as if I was an idiot.

'Lucy! That's such a waste of money!'

'It's not! I've been talking to Kirsti. I've been telling her important stuff.'

I grabbed the phone and ended the call.

'I didn't say goodbye!'

'You're going to have to say goodbye to everyone if you're not careful. They'll put you in prison for stealing phones and running up the world's biggest phone bill.'

She thought about that. 'Would I get to sleep on a bunk bed in prison?'

I phoned Dad on his mobile to explain to him why he couldn't find his landline phone. I tried to make him understand that Lucy misses Kirsti, but he just said, 'Thanks for telling me, Ella. Put Lucy on the phone please.'

He spent a lot longer telling Lucy off than he did thanking me.

Later, I stuffed Amelia's phone down the side of the sofa cushions and when we were watching TV I pretended to find it.

'What's it doing there?' Amelia asked, peeling a squished raisin off the back of it. 'That's not where I left it.'

'It's not really weird that your phone is next to your lounging and complaining spot,' Chloe said.

'What *would* be weird is if it was by the kitchen sink because no one has seen you doing any washing–up for fourteen years.'

Amelia gave Chloe a filthy look. 'I haven't even been alive for fourteen years.'

'Exactly. Even before you were born, you were a shirker.'

They snapped at each other so much that I went up to bed early. Lucy was already asleep, but I could still tell she'd been crying.

CHAPTER 🍓 FIFTEEN

Even though it was Saturday morning, everyone in my house looked miserable. I was worried because Ashandra and Kayleigh hadn't really talked all week. Lucy was sad about Kirsti. Chloe had fallen out with Thunder, but wouldn't tell anyone why. Mum was stressed because she had so much schoolwork to do. Amelia was miserable because that was how she always was. She was also screwing up her face because Chloe was eating yoghurt with a chopstick.

'You don't need to stare,' Chloe said. 'There weren't any clean spoons. Or forks. Or anything except this.'

Amelia kept on staring so Chloe flicked yoghurt at her. Amelia shrieked.

'Girls, please, I'm getting a headache.' Mum

shuffled through one of the many stacks of paper spread out in front of her on the table.

'Are you still worrying about being inspectored?' Lucy asked her. 'You do teaching every day so you can't be that bad at it.'

'I'm not bad at it!' Mum snapped. 'It's just all these stupid rules about how everything ought to be done. They want so many different things included in the lessons that I'm not sure where we're supposed to fit the actual learning part in.'

'Can't you just fill in the lesson plan how they want it to keep them happy?' Chloe asked.

Mum moved a handful of Lucy's plastic dinosaurs off the table. 'I'd have more time to fill in lesson plans if I wasn't always having to pick up after you lot.'

Lucy pouted. 'It's not my fault you haven't done your work!'

'Don't get cheeky with me, young lady!' Mum closed her eyes and took a deep breath. 'You're too little to understand, Lucy,' she said. 'It's not even just about the plans; they expect to see progress from every pupil. Every pupil! What makes them think that they know enough about every pupil to even be able to judge that? Shane Bolton hasn't chewed anything from the craft cupboard for three weeks. That's progress.'

'Sounds like Chloe's kind of boyfriend,' Amelia said.

Chloe pushed Amelia off her chair. 'I'm never having a boyfriend.'

Amelia grabbed Chloe by the legs and pulled her to the floor. The yoghurt and the chopstick went flying.

Then they were rolling over on top of each other and Lucy was squealing and Mum was shouting. We could have been watching cartoons and eating toast; instead, they were all being awful.

I slammed the door. Everybody turned and looked at me.

'Stop it!' I said. 'Everybody, stop being horrible!'

Mum shoved Amelia into one chair and Chloe into another. 'Lucy, get a cloth for that yoghurt.' She pushed her hair back. 'Ella's right. Everyone is getting a bit cross and fed up. I want you all dressed in old clothes in five minutes. We've got a lot of work to do in the garden. No arguments. The fresh air will do us good.'

Surprisingly, everybody did what they were told. We put on old trousers and then we weeded and deadheaded and trimmed and tidied until the garden really looked quite neat.

Mum and Chloe pulled out the picnic table from under the trees and put it in a patch of sunlight so we could eat lunch outside. I helped Mum make a mountain of sandwiches and the others ferried out cups and plates and crisps and tomatoes and apples to the table.

'This is nice, isn't it?' Mum said, looking down at the picnic and around at the garden.

'Brilliant,' Chloe said. And Amelia didn't disagree.

'Lucy, help me fetch the drinks,' Mum said.

I watched Amelia and Chloe sitting next to each other on the bench. It was almost like when they used to sit next to each other all the time and made stupid jokes about who smelt the most. Amelia turned her face up to the sun. Chloe picked up a stray crisp and crunched it happily. Maybe they just needed to get out of the house. Maybe everything was fine between them now—

'Eugh! Chloe, you're revolting!' Amelia said. 'Mum! Chloe's eating food straight off the table and the table's got bird poo on it!'

Chloe glared at Amelia.

'Chloe!' Mum called from the kitchen.

'It's all right, the bird poo is dry,' Chloe called back.

Mum's appeared at the back door. 'It would still be a good idea to use a plate.'

'I was just saying that it's not like the crisps were actually covered in poo.'

Amelia made a vomiting noise.

Chloe picked up another crisp that had fallen out of the packet and on to the table. 'See? It's not dripping with big blobs of gloopy white poop.' Her eyes lit up with an idea. 'Hey, Mum, have we got any mayonnaise?'

'I can look for mayonnaise if you can promise not to ingest anything that's come out of a bird for two minutes.'

'All right.'

Mum and Lucy came back with drinks and chocolate biscuits and mayonnaise.

Chloe shook the mayonnaise jar till a quivering blob sat on her plate. She dipped a crisp in it and crunched it with relish.

Amelia gave her a disgusted look.

Chloe held out the jar to her. 'Do you want some gloopy poop?'

Apart from Amelia and Chloe snapping at each other, it was a nice picnic. It was really good to all chat together about what we could plant in the garden. I did ask Mum if she should be doing her lesson preparation, but she said she could do it later. Overall, I felt quite bright side-ish for the first time in a while.

Even though I managed not to think about Ashandra and Kayleigh for most of the weekend,

I knew I couldn't bear another art lesson with Ash being all tight-lipped and bossy and Kay pretending she didn't care. Anyway, I wanted us to do well with our panel; I'd heard some of the ideas Suvi had suggested for Chloe's class and they sounded really good. So I knew I'd have to talk to my friends.

On Monday, I marched Kayleigh into our tutor room and over to Ashandra. 'Listen,' I said, then I panicked that they'd both be cross with me for interfering, but I was supposed to be acting really nice and sometimes being nice includes doing scary things to help other people sort things out. I took a deep breath. 'Do you think that maybe . . . please could you work together in art? Ash, you're really good at organising and giving people jobs so I think that's what you should concentrate on. And I know you've done some really good research about the things we should include on our panel, but I think you should let Kayleigh talk to everybody about how we're going to actually show that stuff.'

'What do you mean?' Ashandra said. 'We're just going to draw things on and then paint them, aren't we?'

Kayleigh rolled her eyes.

'Why don't you explain your ideas to Ash?' I asked Kayleigh. 'Please.'

'OK.' But she didn't look directly at Ashandra. 'All the tutor groups are going to do painting so we need something different.'

'Something that stands out?' Ashandra was definitely interested.

'Exactly. I thought what if we literally make our panel stand out? A Chinese dragon could be sort of bursting out of it; we could shape the dragon with chicken wire and papier mâché. And the lanterns could be raised too. Maybe with actual lights in, like those little LED ones.'

Ashandra was trying very hard not to look impressed. She wasn't doing a very good job.

'Mmm,' she said. 'That does sound . . . good. How about you describe it to everyone and then I'll divide people up into groups to work on the different parts. OK?'

'OK,' Kayleigh said.

It was definitely progress.

CHAPTER ❧ SIXTEEN

'This is the most revolting thing that has ever happened to me,' Chloe announced, throwing down her mobile phone. It was Wednesday night and we were at Dad's house, lying around the sitting room, waiting for him to get home from work.

Amelia looked up from her magazine. 'I find that hard to believe because you told me only the other day that Buttercup once pooped in your trainers and you wore them all day before you noticed. If something more revolting than that has happened, I don't want to hear about it.'

Lucy was using a toe to make Kirsti's bouncy chair bounce. She stopped for a moment to lean over and look at Chloe's phone, but Chloe snatched it away.

'What is it?' Lucy asked.

Chloe screwed up her face. 'Thunder's sent me a text. He wants me to go to the disco with him.'

'I thought you liked discos,' I said.

'I like dancing and eating crisps and laughing at the teachers' party clothes. I don't like mushy stuff.'

Lucy's eyes went round. 'Does Thunder want to do mushy stuff with you?'

'Urgh!' Amelia groaned. 'Don't put pictures in my head. I'll never be able to eat again if I think about Chloe and Thunder kissing.'

'Does he want to kiss you?' I asked.

Chloe pulled a face. 'If he tries to kiss me, I will tie his lips in a knot. And punch him. A lot.'

'So are you going to say no thanks?'

'No. I'm going to say, "Why on earth did you ask that stupid question? Don't ever ask me a soppy thing like that again or I will pull out your intestines and strangle you with them."'

'That's not very nice,' I said.

Amelia raised her eyebrows. 'If he wants someone who's nice, he's friends with the wrong person.'

'But it must have taken quite a lot of courage to ask you,' I said.

'More like a lot of stupidness.' Chloe puffed out her breath.

'What's happening?' Suvi asked, coming into the room. 'Amelia is pulling a face like I'm asking her to lay the table, but I didn't even do that.'

'Thunder has asked Chloe to the disco,' I said.

I thought Suvi would say, 'That's nice,' in the way that grown-ups do when they don't really get what's going on, but instead Suvi looked at Chloe.

'You don't want to go to the disco with this Thunder?'

'No! He's my friend. All that boyfriend-girlfriend stuff is gross.'

Suvi spread her hands. 'Then tell him this.'

'She can't!' I said. 'He'll be so upset. Why don't you just go with him? It's only one night.'

'It's for you to choose,' Suvi said to Chloe. 'You don't have to do anything you don't want to.'

'Don't worry, she never bothers about other people's feelings,' Amelia snapped from behind her magazine.

Chloe slapped down her phone. 'Fine. I'll tell him no nicely.'

But everyone was still frowning.

Except Lucy. She was blowing raspberries at Kirsti.

Dad wasn't back in time for dinner so we ate without him. I worried about Chloe the whole time I was eating. It's not that I thought that what Amelia said about Chloe not bothering about people's feelings was true; I just wasn't sure that Chloe understood how hard you have to work to be friends with someone.

I volunteered to do the washing-up with Suvi.

'Please can you talk to Chloe?' I asked her. 'I'm afraid she's going to fall out with Thunder.'

Suvi handed me a plate to dry. 'Do you think this boy will stop being friends with Chloe if she says she doesn't want to be his girlfriend?'

I didn't know the answer to that. Thunder and Chloe seemed to have fun together, but wouldn't he be cross if she said no?

Suvi turned to face me. 'I don't think your sister should try to be someone that she is not to make another person happy.'

'But you have to think about other people's feelings! You can't just do whatever you like!' I said.

Suvi thought for a moment. 'Sometimes it's right to make sacrifices for people you care about,' she said. 'But you can't do it every time. And you can't do something that goes against who you are. Chloe doesn't want a boyfriend; if she pretends, it's no good for her *or* Thunder.'

That sort of made sense. 'But how are you

supposed to know when to make sacrifices?' I asked.

Suvi scraped a plate. 'Sometimes you don't. You have to make a balance. There's compromising and then there's standing up for your own feelings and what you believe in.'

'Like you with the squash and the TV.'

Suvi smiled. 'Exactly. I don't want to give up my beliefs on TV, but I want you girls to be happy so I can compromise on the squash.' She put a hand on my shoulder. 'You're a nice girl, Ella.'

That surprised me. I didn't know that Suvi had thought about what kind of girl I am.

She squeezed my shoulder. 'There's squash and there's TV. You have to try to remember the difference. Don't let people put TVs all over your house, Ella.'

Which basically means something else that my nana used to say: Don't let people walk all over you.

Sometimes people say things that you think are probably good advice, but you have absolutely no idea how you could ever actually do them.

CHAPTER ❤ SEVENTEEN

The next day, as we walked into art class, I hoped that the lesson would go smoothly and I wouldn't end up feeling like I was having to compromise things I believe in, like my belief that Ashandra and Kayleigh really should be friends.

In the end, it was a definite improvement, but they weren't exactly working together. Kayleigh explained her ideas for our panel and then Ashandra got people into groups to work on different bits. They hardly spoke to each other, but at least they didn't argue.

On the bright side, Kayleigh came to Hockey Club and we all got changed in the same corner of the changing room without her or Ash saying anything bad.

I was definitely getting better at hockey. Sometimes

the ball went where I wanted it to go. Sometimes I still completely missed it. When we were practising passing in a triangle, I took a big whack at the ball and ended up missing it and spinning right round.

'You're supposed to be playing hockey,' Jasmine said, 'not prancing about.'

And then she hit her ball. Really well.

If I was giving out hockey skills, I wouldn't give them to anyone who couldn't be kind to someone who wasn't as good as them.

I thought that was the end of Jasmine's nasty remarks, but, when I was helping Mrs Henderson collect up all the bibs and balls, she sauntered over and said, 'It's not going to work, you know.'

'What isn't?'

'You keep trying to get your two loser friends to all be loser friends together, but you're forgetting something.'

'What?'

'They hate each other. They could hardly bear being at the same table in art, could they? Which is funny because you'd think that they'd enjoy being sad and stupid together.'

'That's not true,' I said.

She tilted her head and looked at me in such a smug, know-it-all way that I wanted to bash her with a hockey stick.

'It's fine,' I said. 'They're just getting to know each other. Besides, it's none of your business.' And I carried a stack of cones off to the PE cupboard.

When I got to the changing room, Kayleigh and most of the other girls had already gone, but Ashandra was waiting for me. Her fists were clenched.

'Do you know what Kayleigh just called me?' she asked. 'Snooty. She actually called me snooty to my face.'

My shoulders sagged. They didn't really hate each other, did they?

'I'm sure she didn't mean it,' I said.

'She did. I'm not speaking to her again.'

'What about the art competition?'

'It would be all her fault if we lost.' She bit a nail. I knew she didn't want to lose. 'Look,' she said. 'You can be our go-between; you can tell her my plans.'

It seemed like Jasmine was right.

Ashandra picked up her PE bag. 'She's *your* friend, Ella – though I can't see why – you'll just have to sort her out.'

I tried to talk to Kayleigh during history. 'Ashandra's really upset,' I whispered.

'I'm upset too!' she said a lot less quietly. 'She's always going on at me.'

141

'Could you maybe talk to her?'

'No! Listen, Ella, you've got to stop always trying to shove us together. We're too different.'

She didn't speak to me for the rest of the lesson and when the bell went she rushed off. By the time I got to RE, she was already sitting with Nisha from Hockey Club. Ashandra was with Erica; she didn't look up when I walked past her desk. It seemed like they were both cross with me. I didn't understand why. All I'd ever wanted was for everybody to be friends.

Neither of them cared how hard I'd tried to be nice or the effort I'd put into us doing things together.

I was fed up with both of them.

'Did you speak to Thunder?' I asked Chloe that evening while we were watching TV with Lucy.

'Yep.'

'What did you say?'

'I said I didn't want to go to the disco with him.'

'And what did he say?'

'He said, "Oh."'

I was going to ask her what kind of 'Oh', but I'm pretty sure that Chloe doesn't realise that there are different kinds.

'It's fine,' Chloe said. 'I don't know why

everyone else had so much to say about it. I just told him the truth and now everything's back the way it was.'

It all seemed very simple and easy. I didn't quite believe it. I couldn't see how telling someone something they really didn't want to hear would lead to anything but trouble. But before I could ask any more Amelia came in and switched off the TV.

'Move it, you scrapings from the bottom of the pickle jar. There are people capable of intelligent conversation coming round and I don't want them repulsed by the rubbish that comes out of your mouths.'

'What stuff comes out of our mouths?' Lucy asked indignantly.

Amelia pointed at her. 'Nonsense.' She pointed at me. 'Mumbling.' She pointed at Chloe. 'Partially chewed food.'

'It's not like I want any of it to escape!' Chloe said.

'So if you could just retire to the Pit I'd be grateful.' She picked a grubby T-shirt, two mugs and an empty crisp packet off the floor and pushed them into my hands. 'Well, not grateful, but I won't cut anything off while you're sleeping.'

'We can't go to the Pit. Lucy has taped up the door,' I said.

'Why don't you untape it then?'

'Because we're not you,' Chloe said, giving Amelia the evil eye. 'So we respect people's right to Sellotape things up if that's what makes them happy.'

Lucy scowled horribly. 'Yeah, that's what makes me happy.'

'All right, then you can go to the garden, or your bedroom where you can enjoy the scent of cheese and rotten eggs, or you can run into oncoming traffic. In fact, you can choose any place you like as long as it's not here.'

In the end, Chloe went to film Thunder in the bear suit on a roundabout, Lucy headed down to the Pit and closed the door firmly behind her and I hung about in the kitchen, making a cup of tea very slowly.

Amelia's friends arrived. Even though she does say some quite mean things, she seems to have loads. I've seen her at school in a big crowd, but today there were six of them. They're less stampy and jumpy than Chloe's friends, but they still talk quite loudly. When Amelia opened the door to her best friend Lauren, she tutted. 'Are you here again? Why do you keep turning up? Is it because you're desperate for the intellectual stimulation I give you?'

'Actually, it's for the biscuits,' Lauren said.

They laughed.

I finished making my cup of tea and crept down the hallway. I could hear them talking in the sitting room.

'What on earth are you wearing, Milly?' Lauren asked.

I'd seen Milly's flowery dress. I thought it was nice.

'It's vintage,' Milly said.

'It certainly smells vintage,' another girl said.

'No, wait a minute,' Amelia said. 'It is vintage; it reminds me of what my great-aunt Anne was wearing the last time I saw her.'

'Was she one of those really stylish old ladies with diamonds?' Milly asked.

'No, she was living with a million cats and she hadn't changed her clothes since the seventies.'

I winced, but Milly didn't seem to mind. 'You'll be sorry when I set my cat army on you,' she said.

Everybody laughed, including Milly and Amelia.

I sat on the stairs and thought about Amelia. She never seemed to get upset about things like me. If I was more like her, I wouldn't worry about Ash and Kay getting on. Amelia wouldn't let herself end up in the middle of two people being horrible. No one ever hurt Amelia's feelings.

I sighed. I'd tried really hard at being nice and then I'd put lots of effort into using Chloe's way of getting people to be friends (and had the hockey-ball bruises to prove it), but it had all ended up with Ashandra and Kayleigh fighting.

My big sister would never put up with this.

It was time to try Amelia's method and get tough.

CHAPTER ✦ EIGHTEEN

I was really glad I'd decided to be more like Amelia because about seven seconds after I called for Kayleigh the next morning she started moaning about Ashandra again.

'She's a nightmare,' she said. 'I know she's really brainy and sometimes she does say funny stuff, but she's driving me mad. She keeps waving lists in my face and telling me that we're behind schedule for the art project. You've got to talk to her.'

'No,' I said.

'What?'

I could feel my cheeks getting hot. 'No, I'm not talking to her. You talk to her.' I couldn't believe I was saying this stuff, but I must have sounded at least a tiny bit like Amelia because Kayleigh just looked sideways at me and didn't say anything else.

On the way to maths, Ashandra pulled me aside. 'Kayleigh is so frustrating! Tell her that if we don't pick up the pace we're never going to be finished in time. And then we'll lose and I know that doesn't sound like a really big deal, but they'll probably make us wear T-shirts that say "loser" on them for the rest of our school career.'

She was waiting for me to laugh.

'And hats. T-shirts and hats with those little propeller things on,' she added, looking less sure of herself.

Even though that was quite a funny image, I didn't laugh.

'So can you tell Kayleigh that we've got to get a move on?'

I bit my lip. 'No,' I said.

'What do you mean no? Don't you want us to win this competition?'

'Of course I do.' Then I remembered Amelia never admits to caring about anything. 'But it's not my problem,' I said. 'You two need to talk to Miss Gardner.'

Ashandra stared at me. Eventually, she said, 'Maybe you're right.'

It was amazing. No wonder Amelia was always bossing people about. If you say something like you mean it, people actually pay attention.

When we got to maths, we discovered that Mr Garibaldi (or Mr Very-Baldie as Jasmine calls him) had done a seating plan. It's not a good sign when teachers do that because it means they have Had Enough and are about to get really bossy and Kieran is going to be kept in at lunchtime. Nobody was very happy about the plan. Ashandra and Kayleigh were put next to each other; if I'd been caring about things, I would have been pleased, but they both looked horrified.

Amazingly, even though they didn't speak to each other for the whole of maths, Ashandra and Kayleigh went off at breaktime to speak to Miss Gardner. I went too, but I tried to look like I was just there in a casual way and not because I was desperate for them to sort things out. Amelia never looks desperate.

'Miss Gardner?' Ashandra said. 'We're having some problems.'

Miss Gardner looked up from her laptop.

'What sort of problems?'

'About us being the coordinators,' Kayleigh said.

'Really?' Miss Gardner walked over to our panel and pulled the cover off. 'I thought you were progressing well yesterday. I like the pagoda.'

Ashandra nodded. 'That's the Fogong Temple Pagoda.' She hesitated. 'It was Kayleigh's idea to use lolly sticks for the wood effect.'

149

Kayleigh looked at her. 'Ashandra made the people who are good at fiddly things stick them on while the rest of us were working on the dragon's head.'

'I love the idea of the dragon's head; it really makes your piece original.' Miss Gardner studied the panel some more.

'It's looking really good, isn't it?' I said.

'But we keep having arguments,' Kayleigh said.

'Perhaps you could carry on with this great work, but skip the arguments,' Miss Gardner suggested.

They didn't look sure.

'Do you know why I chose you two to be in charge?' she asked them.

'I do,' I said because I was being tough and bold and Amelia never minds answering questions that aren't exactly addressed to her. 'Ashandra is good at sorting out things and people, and Kayleigh is really creative.'

'Exactly, Ella. And it seems to me that you're using those skills well. Maybe you just need to appreciate what the other person is bringing to this project.'

Ashandra frowned and Kayleigh looked at her shoes.

'Kayleigh told me that you're really good at getting people working,' I said to Ashandra.

Kayleigh shrugged, but I could see that Ash was pleased. I turned to her. 'And don't you think the way Kay moulded that dragon's head is amazing?'

'I suppose,' Ash said. 'It does look pretty good.'

'I think you're going to get better and better at working as a team,' Miss Gardner said.

Ash and Kay seemed to believe her.

I thought about what Miss Gardner had said while we were waiting for Miss Espinoza to take afternoon registration. It just goes to show that getting tough was a good idea. Although Ash and Kay still weren't exactly chatty. Kay was hurriedly trying to finish her history homework before the next lesson and Ash was over at Erica's desk.

I wondered if she was telling her about our chat with Miss Gardner. I tried to work out what she was saying from her face, but Jasmine blocked my view by climbing on a desk and starting to bend over backwards like that woman Lucy loves on *Secrets of Magic* who can fit herself into a tiny box. Jasmine went completely over into a bridge; she didn't even put her hands out until the last minute. It was quite impressive. Then she pushed off with her legs and flipped over into a standing position again. All on top of a tiny table. It was amazing, but Amelia never says anything is amazing so I didn't either. Jasmine's friends did though; they all started cooing and telling her how fantastic she is.

Jasmine smirked. 'Mrs Henderson says I'm the most talented gymnast this school has ever had.'

And then it happened. I just opened my mouth and out it came.

'That's funny because everybody else says that you're the most big-headed idiot this school has ever had.'

Courtney sucked in her breath and everyone else laughed. I hadn't even realised anyone else was listening.

'Good one,' Ashandra said.

Jasmine's eyes were boring into me. 'You're jealous. Just wait till I'm at the Olympics.'

The room was completely quiet; they were all waiting to hear what I would say back. I said exactly what I knew Amelia would say.

'I think you're confused. There isn't an event for selfish show-offs at the Olympics. But you'd definitely get the gold if there was.'

Jasmine was red in the face. She opened her mouth to say something awful back, but Miss Espinoza walked in and everyone had to sit down.

My heart was thumping, but it felt good not to be the one made to look stupid for once.

CHAPTER ✿ NINETEEN

On Friday, things between Ashandra and Kayleigh seemed to even out to a sort of frosty politeness. But at home things between Amelia and Chloe just got worse and worse. On Saturday morning, Dad came back from dropping Lucy off at ballet and he and Suvi took Kirsti upstairs to get her changed and dressed. That's when Amelia and Chloe started snapping at each other again.

Chloe was disappointed because Thunder had backed out of their plan to film Big Bear on roller skates.

'What could possibly be more important than this?' she asked me.

'Maybe he has to do something with his parents,' I said.

'Maybe he doesn't want to see you because

you crushed him when he asked you out,' Amelia said.

'Don't be stupid,' Chloe said.

But it was true that Thunder had been making excuses not to see Chloe recently. She frowned.

Amelia started humming the song she'd written for International Day.

Chloe groaned. 'Not that rubbish again.'

Amelia stopped humming and started singing.

Chloe put her fingers in her ears. 'You do realise that no one is going to want to listen to you warbling on about countries in harmony and all that rubbish.'

Upstairs, Kirsti started howling.

'You sound just like her,' Chloe said. 'No wonder Dad isn't coming to see you sing; he has to put up with enough wailing already.'

'Shut your face.' Amelia shoved Chloe in the chest.

Chloe pushed her back. 'You shut it. You think you're so brilliant just because you can sing and you read books and wear make-up.'

'You're just jealous. Maybe in a million years you'll act like an adult.'

'I'm not jealous! You think you're so big, but you're an idiot, always being sarky with Dad and pretending you're not part of this family.'

'What family?' Amelia exploded. 'We're not a proper family! Mum and Dad barely even talk to each other.'

'So? He's still our dad.'

Amelia looked at Chloe with dagger eyes. 'We all know that you're on his side.'

'What do you mean, on his side?'

'You think he's brilliant. You're always throwing your arms round him. You never even consider Mum. What do you think it's like when someone you love goes off with another woman and leaves you behind to cope, and five minutes later they've got a whole new life with their new baby, and they don't care about you any more and they never even show up to hear you sing?' She pushed past me and ran out of the room.

Chloe's forehead creased. 'Wait a minute,' she called to Amelia's back. 'Are we talking about Mum or you?'

I don't think Amelia really knew.

'Did I hear shouting?' Dad asked when he came downstairs a few minutes later with Kirsti on his arm.

Chloe shrugged.

I was being tough so it wasn't up to me to explain everything. I stared at my juice. In a tough way.

'Well, let's try not to get too boisterous at this time in the morning; we've already had Lucy doing the fairy elephant dance on the way to ballet,' Dad said, popping Kirsti in her bouncy chair. 'And I know Kirsti's been bellowing, but we should try not to disturb the neighbours any more than necessary.'

I knew that when you've got Kirsti howling in your ear it's hard to hear anything else, but I was surprised he didn't want to know what the shouting was about.

Chloe didn't seem bothered about telling him. 'What's the Plan for this morning?' she asked.

'The Plan is for everybody to be really good and quiet while I get some work done. We might have time for half an hour's fishing this afternoon,' Dad said, picking up his phone and starting to look through his emails.

'I'm going to tell Thunder to stop being an idiot then.' Chloe attempted to moonwalk out of the kitchen. I stood up to follow her.

'Tell Amelia we're not going out this morning, will you, Ella?' Dad asked, not looking up from his phone.

'I think she might have locked herself in the bathroom again.'

Dad looked up from his phone and then back

down again. 'Amelia and Chloe seem to be winding each other up a bit today. They're normally such good pals. Do you think you could smooth things over between them?'

Suddenly, I understood a bit why Amelia was so cross with him. How could he possibly have not noticed that Amelia and Chloe didn't get on at all any more?

'They always wind each other up; they fell out ages ago,' I said. 'They hardly talk to each other at the moment. And even when they do it's just to say nasty things.'

'Mmm,' Dad said, still looking at his stupid emails. He wasn't paying attention to me. I didn't care though because I was being tough. Which was good because it isn't very nice when your dad doesn't listen to something important you're telling him.

It wasn't a very good weekend. We didn't even go fishing. Dad only came out of his study to watch the football with Chloe. Amelia only came out of the bathroom to shout at people.

CHAPTER ✿ TWENTY

By Tuesday, Chloe was still staying as far away from Amelia as possible so I was keeping her company in the forest at the bottom of the garden while she sketched a tree for her art homework. She was eating a packet of Monster Munch at the same time. I don't know where she got them. I could only find boring ready salted crisps in the cupboard.

'Are Ashandra and Kayleigh friends now that you're all in Hockey Club?' Chloe asked.

I shook my head. I didn't have the energy to tell her that playing on a team together didn't seem to have worked and neither did being nice. The bright side of me being tough now was that at least Ash and Kay seemed to understand that I didn't want to hear them complaining about each other, even if they were still pretty frosty with each other, only speaking about the project when they had to. To be honest, I didn't feel very tough or strong about the whole thing. I tried to squish down my worries. Amelia wouldn't let this kind of thing bother her.

'Not exactly friends,' I said.

The weather wasn't as warm as it had been so Chloe had brought out a flask of tea. She poured me another cup and held out her crisp packet to me. 'Try a mouthful with a Monster Munch; it makes them sort of fizz.' Then she frowned. She doesn't normally frown when she's talking about crisps.

'Are you all right?' I asked.

'Mmm. I've been thinking.'

That sounded serious. Chloe doesn't like to think about things if she can help it.

She sighed. 'I don't really understand all that stuff Amelia was saying about Mum and Dad.'

'Me neither.'

'Do you think I'm upsetting Mum?'

'No.' I hesitated. 'I don't think so . . . I don't know.'

Then she said something that proves what I'm always saying about Chloe being much more sensible than people think.

'Let's ask Mum.'

She packed up the flask and her sketch stuff and we went into the kitchen where Mum was making dinner.

'Mum, can I ask you something?' Chloe twisted one leg round the other.

'Of course.'

Chloe opened her mouth and shut it again. Her neck was pink. Usually when Chloe talks the words tumble out. She always has something to say.

Mum put down the cheese grater and leant across the counter towards Chloe. When you know someone really well, their quiet bits can tell you as much as their words. Mum knew something was wrong.

'What is it, sweetheart?' she asked.

'Do you want me to stop hugging Dad?'

I was sure that Amelia was wrong and that Mum would just laugh, but she didn't.

'Of course not. Why on earth would you think that?'

'Amelia says I should be on your side.'

I've noticed that sometimes grown-ups do this face when you speak to them, and you know that you've said something that's shocked or upset them, even though you don't know why.

Mum bit her lip. 'Ella, do you think you could

fetch your sisters? Wait, Lucy is at Rose's house. Just find Amelia.'

Chloe shot me a look; she didn't get it either.

When I came back with Amelia, Mum made us all sit down at the table.

'Girls, do you remember when Dad and I told you we were getting divorced?'

I blinked. Even though it was nearly a year and a half ago, I did remember. It was a horrible, horrible day.

'We said that the most important thing was that you remember that we love you all very much.'

'Yeah,' Amelia said. 'But what's that got to do with you hating Dad?'

Mum actually gasped. I nearly did too because I'd never thought that about Mum and Dad.

'Amelia! I don't hate your father. I've never even said a bad word about him.'

'That's because you never finish a sentence about him,' Amelia said.

That's sort of true. Mum doesn't say much about Dad. Or Suvi or Kirsti.

'And you cried when you two got divorced.'

Mum pinched the top of her nose.

'I did cry,' she said slowly. 'Getting divorced is sad and difficult and it can make you cry, but that doesn't mean I hate your dad.' She looked right into Amelia's eyes. 'I don't. And I certainly don't want you to take sides. There aren't sides,' Mum insisted. 'We're all on the same side.'

Amelia slapped a hand down on the table. 'No we're not! He went off! He left us!'

'And I think maybe I should have realised just how angry that's made you,' Mum said softly.

'I'm angry for you.'

I stared at Amelia. Her voice was all gravelly and choked.

Mum slid her chair closer to Amelia and wrapped an arm round her. 'You don't have to worry about me. I'm fine. I'm very happy with our life.'

Amelia was crying. Chloe widened her eyes at me. We hadn't seen Amelia cry for a very long time.

'You're allowed to be angry with Dad for yourself,' Mum said to Amelia. 'You all are.'

Amelia wiped her nose with the back of her hand. 'I'm angry with everybody. It's not fair.'

Amelia cried and cried. Mum shushed her and rocked her like she was tiny.

Chloe squeezed my hand.

I bit the inside of my cheek and tried to think tough things.

CHAPTER ✦TWENTY-ONE

Ever since Mr Garibaldi made them sit together, I'd been watching Ashandra's and Kayleigh's backs in maths. At first, they completely ignored each other. It was as if there was an invisible line down the middle of the table and they were very careful not to let even an elbow cross it. But then, during our double lesson, while I was bent over my book, out of the corner of my eye, I saw Ashandra turn round to look at me. Then she turned back and said something to Kayleigh. After that, I saw them whispering several times.

After the next lesson, Kayleigh even waved to Ashandra when she went off to talk to Erica. Me and Kayleigh got in the queue for the vending machines.

'So . . . I was just chatting to Ashandra,' Kayleigh said.

My heart did a little squeeze, but you can't get excited about things because that's when people crush your hopes so I just said, 'Oh.'

'You never said she liked horses.'

That wasn't what I was expecting her to say. 'I didn't know she did.'

'Well, mostly she's just read books about them – she's going to lend me some – but she wants to start riding lessons so she's going to go with me to the stables on Saturday. You'll come, won't you?'

When Kayleigh and I were little, we used to play 'horses' in the playground a lot. At first, I didn't know what to do and I felt silly, but Kayleigh said I could be called Spirit and she made trotting about look so much fun that soon we were galloping through meadows and up mountains every playtime. I loved it. I did try going to the stables with Kayleigh for one lesson, but, when I found out that none of the horses were called things like Sparkle Hooves and they didn't have glitter in their manes and actually they were quite stampy and toothy, I wasn't so keen. But it had been ages since I tried it and maybe all of us riding around together was the way to finally make us best friends.

'If you like,' I said, trying to stay tough. But then I completely couldn't help adding, 'I can't wait.'

*

Whenever I tell my mum about my day, she always knows what the most important bit is.

'So Ashandra and Kayleigh actually decided they wanted to do something together?' she asked when I told her about the horse riding.

I nodded.

'That's excellent. I'm really pleased. I know how much you want them to get along.'

'Do you think we can be best friends now?'

She smoothed the hair out of my eyes. 'I hope you can all be friends, Ella. But remember, you've got to give it time. And there are different kinds of friends; as long as everybody's happy, that's the most important thing.'

She squeezed my arm. 'Which reminds me.' She looked over at Amelia and Chloe watching TV.

'I want to talk to you all. Where's Lucy?'

'She's in the Pit,' I said.

'She's always down there now,' Chloe said.

'Do you know what she's doing?' Mum asked.

Amelia shrugged. 'She's probably amassing an army of headless dolls to attack us in the night.'

'Actually,' Chloe said, "if you were going to make an army, probably one with heads would be better. Then they could see what they were attacking.'

Amelia sniffed. 'Lucy should have thought about that before she popped their heads off.'

Lucy walked into the sitting room.

'What have you been doing, sweetheart?' Mum asked.

Lucy thought for a second. Even though she's only seven, she's already way too smart to say 'nothing' so she said, 'I was building a Lego dungeon for one of my dinosaurs. He was visiting the Sylvanian school, but he went crazy and chewed one of the baby rabbits so I had to lock him away.'

Which sounded quite believable for Lucy, but I still thought she was up to something.

'Anyway, I wanted to speak to you all,' Mum said. 'Chloe, turn the TV off.'

Chloe zapped it with the remote.

'Lucy, last night I told your sisters that I don't hate your dad and that nobody needs to take sides.'

I expected Lucy to ask a lot of questions, but instead she said, 'I know that already.'

'Good. But we need to talk about one more thing,' Mum said. 'I also said last night that I'm happy and I really meant it. I don't want you to think that your dad "ran off" and I was the one left behind.'

'But you'd still be together if it wasn't for Suvi,' Amelia said.

That wasn't true, was it?

Mum looked serious. 'No,' she said. 'That's not how it is. Dad didn't even meet Suvi until after he'd moved out.'

Amelia pouted. 'Well, it was all pretty quick, wasn't it? A year and a half ago you two were still married; now Dad's got a whole new family!'

'Sometimes these things happen quickly and I know you haven't had much time to get used to the idea.'

'Maybe, if Dad hadn't rushed into things with Suvi, you and him might have got back together.'

Mum looked round at us and I realised that we were all dead still, waiting to see what she would say to that.

'Oh, girls, I'm so sorry that this is so difficult for you. But I need you to understand what really happened.' She looked at each of us in turn. 'We made a decision, your father and I, both of us together, that we didn't want to be married any more. It wasn't anything to do with anybody else and we were never going to get back together whether Suvi had come along or not.'

It felt a little bit like things finishing all over again. It's not like I'd exactly thought my parents would get back together, but Mum saying it would never happen still made my chest go all tight.

Mum squeezed Amelia's hand. 'Dad didn't

abandon me and he didn't abandon you girls. He wants to see you as much as he can.'

'So why does he work so much?' Amelia asked.

Mum's forehead creased. 'Work is important to your father; it's . . . it's to do with how he grew up, but you should know that you girls come first.'

Amelia tried to interrupt, but Mum went on.

'Even if he misses things sometimes, even if he's late, when you really get down to it, you girls are the most important thing in the world to him.'

'How do you know?' Lucy asked.

'Because I feel the same way. Because it's the one thing that we are in complete agreement on,' Mum said and pulled us all into a big Strawberry Girls hug.

CHAPTER ♥ TWENTY-TWO

Ashandra leant me one of her books about ponies. I loved it when the girl in the story, Penny, was chasing the thief and she was urging her pony to go faster through the moonlit field. They went soaring over the stream, moving as one. It sounded almost like flying.

The couple of times that I've actually been riding were a lot more . . . bumpy. You're supposed to get into the rhythm of the movement, but I ended up feeling like I was sitting on a washing machine. A washing machine with very long legs. Horses are much bigger than you think.

As soon as we got to the stables on Saturday morning, Kayleigh was whispering away to her special horse friend, Misty. You could tell that Misty was pleased to see her. My problem is that

I don't speak Horse. I don't even know how to be around them. I go all stiff and worry that they know that I'm afraid. Like dogs or teachers.

Ashandra was brilliant. Even though it was her first time, she wasn't scared at all. She did what Kayleigh did and asked lots of questions and some things she just seemed to do naturally. Ashandra never looks uncomfortable; it's one of the things I like best about her. She always seems to know what to do and usually that makes me feel better too.

I hoped that I would get a white horse called Moonlight or a black one called Raven, but when Kayleigh's mum led out my horse he was brown and his name was Oscar. He looked at me and pulled back his lips to show me what he thought of me.

'Ah,' Ashandra said. 'He's smiling at you.'

Ashandra never thinks animals want to bite her either.

First, we got the horses ready, then we went for what the teacher lady called 'a nice gentle round and round'. Which meant following each other in a circle in a big field.

I wasn't exactly enjoying myself because of the jolting and the quite-far-from-the-groundness, but Ash and Kay were chatting and the sun was shining and there were some little purple flowers in the hedge, and I thought if I could just keep a good grip on the reins I might make it to the end of the lesson.

Then there was a loud bang from somewhere back near the stables. Oscar flinched and for a split second I really thought he was going to bolt. He didn't, but in my mind he tore across the field with me desperately clinging on, then he jerked me off his back and I got tangled up in his powerful, stomping legs.

After that, I couldn't concentrate on purple flowers. I just clung on and tried not to imagine a hoof in the face.

When we finally got off, I was proud of myself for not making a fuss, but my legs felt a bit like they do when you get off a boat.

'That was awesome,' Ashandra said.

Mum was waiting in the car with Chloe. She offered Kayleigh and Ashandra a lift, but Kay was staying for an advanced lesson and Ash's mum was already pulling into the driveway.

'How did it go?' Chloe asked as I climbed in next to her.

'It was great. Ashandra and Kayleigh were chatting the whole time. Ash is going to lend Kayleigh some more of her pony books and

Kayleigh is going to show Ash how to do a fancy plait in a horse's tail.'

'Did you like riding?' Mum asked.

'No, it was horrible. Horses are totally unpredictable and you never know what they're going to do next, but that's OK.'

'I'm sorry you didn't enjoy it,' Mum said. 'At least you gave it a try. You don't have to go again.'

I didn't think Mum understood the point of going riding. It didn't matter if I was completely terrified as long as Ashandra and Kayleigh were getting on. If they could have fun riding together, it wouldn't be long until we were all best friends.

'What have you been doing?' I asked Chloe.

'Me and Thunder were going to film Big Bear shopping. He was supposed to knock a load of bags of flour off the shelf.'

She didn't smile, even though she loves things falling off other things.

'Didn't it go well?'

'Thunder was being an idiot.'

'Why?'

'He wouldn't do it properly. He didn't make any good suggestions and then, before we'd even got to the flour bit, he said he had to go.'

I didn't know what to say. It seemed like things

between Thunder and Chloe weren't as fine as she'd said they were.

I dropped my voice and leant closer to Chloe. Mum was listening to the radio. 'Do you think maybe he feels a bit embarrassed?' I asked.

'Why would he feel embarrassed?'

'You know, because he asked you out and you said no.'

Chloe wrinkled her nose. 'But . . . I mean, what's the point in being funny about that? It was ages ago.'

Some people don't worry about things very much. It's hard to explain to them that other people worry about things a lot.

'I'd be embarrassed if it was me,' I said. 'And maybe a bit hurt.'

She looked at me for a long time, like she was trying to unravel a clue.

'If it was you, what would you want the person who'd said no to you to do?'

'I don't know. I'd just be worried that they thought I was stupid and that they didn't like me.'

'Of course I still like him! Even if it was a bit stupid.'

'I think you should tell him that. The first bit, not the second bit.'

She blew her fringe off her forehead. 'I don't

know why people can't accept things the way they are. You have to just get over it.'

'Sometimes people need to talk about stuff a bit.'

'I'm not very good at talking.'

'You're better than you think you are. Anyway, it's not exactly about what you say; it's the fact that you're doing it.'

She shrugged. 'I guess I could try.'

When we got home, I did my maths homework. I find it really calming when I'm working through a page of sums; it's nice knowing exactly what to do and where the sum is going.

Basically, the bright side of maths homework is that it isn't at all like a horse.

CHAPTER ❤TWENTY-THREE

On Monday night, Kayleigh rang me. I could tell from the background noise that she was outside.

'Where are you?' I asked.

'Ashandra and me have been shopping,' she said. 'We've got these brilliant little lights for the lanterns.'

'Lanterns?'

'You know, for our panel? For the art competition?'

'Oh.'

'They're like tealights, but with a battery instead of a flame. I think they'll look brilliant. Miss Gardner said they didn't have anything like that in the art department so we decided we should just look ourselves.'

I wondered when all this deciding had gone on because I hadn't heard anything about it before.

'So we're finished now,' she went on. 'And Ash's mum is going to take us for pizza. She said we should ring and invite you.'

Did that mean that Ash and Kay hadn't thought about inviting me themselves?

'Um . . . I have to ask my mum.'

'Well, Ash's mum wants to stop at the chemist's so we're going to be at Pizza Hut in about half an hour. Ring me back if you can come.'

I put the phone down. I knew that someone who is looking on the bright side wouldn't worry about when exactly Ash and Kay planned this, and why they were only inviting me at the last minute, so I tried not to worry about it either.

Mum was in the kitchen, staring at the table. At least, I knew it was the table, but you actually couldn't see very much of it. It was covered with piles of unopened post, Amelia's books and crumby plates. There were also crayons, a half-eaten banana, six different bottles of nail varnish and Lucy's recorder. Mum looked up at me. 'Susan's coming round to help me with my long-term planning,' she said. 'And I don't even know where she can sit.'

I looked at the chairs. They were completely covered too. A stack of textbooks on one, Chloe's football boots on another and a damp sheet draped across the other two.

'What about in the sitting room?' I asked.

'It's worse. Lucy's made some sort of jungle scene on the table in there. There are loo-roll trees and plastic animals everywhere.'

'This isn't that bad,' I said. 'We can clear it up.'

Mum looked round the kitchen and sighed. It wasn't just the table and chairs. The sink was full of dishes; the counter was covered in crumbs and jam smears. The nice china on the dresser was hidden by things that shouldn't have been there like Amelia's hair-straighteners, a broken lamp and an army of monster figures arranged as if they were about to attack the teapot. None of the cupboards were closed. Pasta spilled out of one and saucepans out of another. There were grubby tea towels hanging from doorknobs, and the top of the cooker had baked-on brown stuff. I was so used to it that my messy alarm didn't go off every time I came into the room, but, if you weren't used to it, it did look a bit of a state.

Mum squared her shoulders. 'I just have to give it a quick going-over and hope Susan isn't too appalled.' She started stacking plates. 'What did you want, love?'

I knew I was supposed to have given up being nice and caring about other people, but I didn't want to go off and eat pizza while my mum was having a hard time. Even when my mum is cross or tired, she always helps us with things. I also knew that that was the whole reason the kitchen was a mess. She'd spent Sunday helping Chloe with her volcanoes project and most of Saturday shopping for a new party dress for Lucy.

There's no way I could ever pretend to be tough with my mum. Which was a relief because, when you're trying to be one thing or not to be something else, you have to spend a lot of time worrying about what to do. When you're with someone that you can't pretend with, you just do the thing you feel. And I felt like I wanted to help Mum.

'I haven't got anything to do,' I lied. 'So I can do the tidying while you do the washing-up.'

'Oh, Ella, you're an angel. I don't know where the weekend disappeared to and I let Amelia off the washing-up last night because I thought it would do her good to go out with Lauren.'

Before we started, I sent Kayleigh a quick text to say that I couldn't make it. But I didn't waste time worrying if they would miss me. Instead, I tidied and scrubbed really fast and, by the time Mum's friend Susan arrived, the kitchen looked completely presentable. Mum gave me a big hug when we'd finished.

*

The next day Ashandra and Kayleigh proudly showed me the tiny lights that they'd got for the lanterns.

'My mum said the batteries should last for hours so we can switch them on before the parents arrive on International Day,' Ashandra said.

'They're great. It'll look fantastic,' I said.

And I really meant it. The panel was going to be fantastic and it was fantastic that Ash and Kay were getting on. And, even though I'd missed out on pizza and Ash telling her funny stories, I was still glad that I'd helped my mum.

I didn't care what Mrs Bottomley said; it's nice to be nice.

CHAPTER ♥ TWENTY-FOUR

At lunchtime on Wednesday, Amelia and Chloe appeared at my table. It was a surprise to see them standing together without one of them bashing the other one. Chloe was eating a pork chop. I don't know where she got it from. They weren't on the menu.

'I got a text from Mum,' Amelia said.

Immediately, a whole load of terrible things piled into my mind. 'What's happened?' I could barely get the words out.

'The inspectors have arrived.'

That's when I realised that Mum probably wouldn't tell us about a car crash or the house blowing up by text. The inspectors were pretty bad news though.

'Poor Mum,' I said. 'Did she say anything else?'

Chloe shook her head. 'Nope. Amelia asked her if she wanted us to come home tonight instead of going to Dad's, but Mum said she'd be fine.'

I had visions of Mum working through the night. 'I hope she remembers to eat something,' I said.

'She'll get more done without us there,' Amelia said.

'Do you think she'll be all right?' Chloe asked.

'She'll be fine, you turnips!' Amelia said, but in a sort of nice way.

She didn't even say anything mean to Chloe. I didn't know whether to be comforted by that or afraid.

We all rushed home from school to Dad's house. Suvi had already picked up Lucy, who was playing with Kirsti on her mat.

'Come upstairs,' Chloe whispered to Lucy. 'We're having a sisters' meeting.'

'Then Kirsti has to come; she's our sister too.'

'Don't be silly, Lucy,' I said. 'Kirsti's just a baby. Besides, this is about Mum.'

Lucy didn't look too happy, but she followed us upstairs anyway.

In our bedroom, Amelia explained about the inspectors to Lucy. Since Amelia cried all over Mum, she's been a lot more patient with Lucy and much less shouty with the rest of us.

'Shall we go to Mum's school and beat the inspectors up?' Lucy asked.

'Don't be ridiculous,' Amelia said, but I think Chloe was definitely considering it.

'Will it be OK?' Lucy asked.

Amelia nodded. 'Mum's a good teacher and the inspectors will be able to see that. They're just observing her. They're not going to do anything terrible to her. Anyway, at least now that they're here it will all be over by tomorrow night.'

'We should do something nice when it's finished,' I said.

Lucy did a somersault on her bed. 'We should have a Whoopee!'

A Whoopee is a celebration. In our family, when someone does something good like getting a swimming certificate or managing to pass their ballet exam, even though they did call the examiner a big pig, everyone decorates that person's bedroom and makes them a present and says 'whoopee' a lot. We haven't had one for ages. There's not been much to celebrate, I suppose.

'Do we really need to make stupid noises to

congratulate someone?' Amelia asked, sounding more like her old, impatient self.

'I've got a noise to congratulate you on being such a moaner,' Chloe said and she did a ginormous fart.

'Gross!'

I could see that Amelia was going to say no to the celebration idea so I was preparing myself to be tough and not mind, but Lucy is very good at getting people to do things.

She looked Amelia up and down. 'Amelia's too big for a Whoopee.'

That was exactly the right thing to say because Amelia hates being told she can't do things.

Amelia stuck out her chin. 'I'm willing to participate if it's tastefully done.'

'That means she'll do it if she can boss us about,' Chloe said.

'She does that anyway,' Lucy said.

Amelia took a notepad out of her bag and started writing a list.

'If it's going to be tomorrow after the inspection is finished, we have to sort out decorations and presents tonight.'

'I'm going to do a really good present,' Lucy said. 'Who can give me some money?'

'Presents are supposed to be home-made, remember?' I said.

Lucy put her hands on her hips. 'I know that, but I need to buy the things to make it out of.'

'We're going to have to go shopping,' Chloe said.

We stared at each other. Amelia and Chloe are allowed to go into town by themselves. Lucy and me aren't.

Lucy sensed she was about to be left behind. 'No way! I need to come. I need to get things.'

'Tell us what you want and we'll get them,' Chloe said.

'I don't know exactly what they are yet! I have to see things; you can't do it for me, you don't have my . . . my visions! My visions of a completely delightful present.'

We burst out laughing.

'Shut up!' Lucy said and she kicked Chloe in the shins.

'You can't come,' Amelia said. 'We'd need an adult for us all to go. Dad's not back yet and he probably won't be for ages.'

'We could ask Suvi,' I said quietly.

'No,' Amelia snapped. 'This isn't anything to do with her. This is for Mum.'

'She doesn't have to be part of it. We could just ask her to drive us.'

It took me ten minutes to persuade Amelia and, in the end, it was only because she was convinced that Suvi would say no that she said I could ask if I really wanted to.

'But don't tell her everything,' Amelia said. 'This is our business.'

So I went downstairs.

'Suvi?'

She was bouncing Kirsti on her lap.

'Yes.'

'Can I ask you a favour?'

'Sure.'

'It's sort of a secret, but we need to go to the shops. It's because M—'

'Stop.' Suvi held up a hand. 'Don't tell me more if it's a secret. I can take you to the shops.'

'All of us?'

That surprised her. 'OK.' Her face clouded. 'Except we won't all fit in my car; it's even smaller than your father's.'

'I could stay behind,' I said.

'No, no one is getting left behind,' Suvi said. And I was glad she did.

So we took the bus. We went to the shopping centre on the edge of town. First, we went in the big hobby shop to get art supplies and then in the massive supermarket to buy cake ingredients.

When we got back, Dad still wasn't home. Suvi checked her phone.

'He's going to be very late again,' she said.

Lucy gathered up the crêpe paper and glue she'd made Amelia buy for her.

'Can I make this in your bedroom where no one can see?' she asked Suvi.

'Yes,' Suvi said.

'You're not very nosy for a grown-up,' Lucy said.

Suvi seemed to appreciate that this was a compliment.

'Are you sure it's OK for her to use your room?' I asked. 'What if she gets glue on the carpet or pen on the duvet cover?'

'If Lucy gets any mess anywhere, she will scrub the stains out of course.'

I watched Lucy take this in. She nodded to Suvi and walked upstairs with great dignity.

'Bet she doesn't spill a drop,' Chloe said.

Suvi handles things in a completely different way to my mum or my dad, but it's quite effective.

When Lucy came to find us in our bedroom where we were making bunting from flowery wrapping paper, she had something behind her back.

'Ta-dah!' And she held up a flower made out of pipe cleaners and crêpe paper.

'Wow, Lucy,' Chloe said. 'That is actually really nice.'

'Why do you sound so surprised? You sound like Mrs Horton when she's telling me that I'm allowed to go out to play for once because I've behaved in the lesson.' She screwed up her nose. 'Or at least I think that's what she sounds like. She hasn't said it for a long time.'

'Chloe just means that it's a lovely flower,' I said.

Lucy pouted. 'It's not a flower.'

'Really? Because it's a good one,' Chloe said.

'It's not a flower.'

I took a closer look. 'But it's got petals and a stem and leaves and everything. What is it then?'

'It's a bee swatter.'

Amelia looked up from her snipping. 'A bee swatter? Seriously?'

'Yes,' said Lucy in a voice that was stretched out tight like a rubber band. 'You put a bit of honey in here.' She pointed to the top of the rolled-up stem. 'And the bee sniffs it.' She mimed a sniffing bee. 'And you keep very quiet.' She dropped her voice to a whisper. 'And he crawls in and then when he's inside you go . . . WHACK! WHACK! WHACK!' She slapped the flower hard against the bed. 'And your bee problem is solved.'

Amelia bit her lip. Chloe squeezed her mouth shut and looked out of the window.

'So what's with the petals?' I asked in a voice with only a tiny wobble of a laugh in it.

'Obviously, it looks like a flower so you can lure the bee in.'

A snort escaped from Amelia. 'Lucy, for a seven-year-old, you use the word "lure" far too much.'

'Still looks like a flower to me,' Chloe said.

'That's because you've got the brains of a bee,' Lucy said.

Chloe stuck her tongue out.

'Mum can use it as a flower,' I said to Chloe. 'She can put in a vase on the mantelpiece.'

Lucy scowled. 'She can if she wants people to say, "Why have you got that bee swatter in a vase?"' She gently wrapped her creation in some of the flowery wrapping paper and stuck it down with a piece of Sellotape bitten off with her teeth. 'Urgh, can we get some strawberry-flavoured Sellotape?'

'They don't make strawberry Sellotape,' Amelia said.

'Yes they do. I saw it in the shop; it's got little pictures of strawberries on.'

'What do you think my Hello Kitty tape tastes of?' I asked. 'Cat?'

'Probably.'

'What does cat taste like?' Chloe asked.

'Fluffy.' And Lucy scooped up her bee swatter parcel and flounced out of the room.

'She would know,' Amelia said. 'Remember when next-door's cat bit her? She bit it back.'

When we'd finished the decorations, we moved on to our presents. Amelia locked herself in the bathroom so I didn't know what she was doing. Chloe made a bead bracelet for Mum. She always makes bead bracelets for Whoopees, but she chooses all the different beads to mean something so it's extra cool. She used a handful of smiley-face beads to represent Mum's pupils and in the middle she put a big gold-star bead to show what a good teacher Mum is.

'That's original,' Amelia said when she came out of the bathroom and saw that Chloe was making her usual bracelet present. She hasn't completely given up saying rude, sarcastic things.

'Just because you've chucked away all the bracelets I worked hard to make for you,' Chloe said.

'Look, Amelia,' I interrupted. 'I've made Mum some more marking labels.'

I'd thought really hard about a present that would be useful to Mum. So I used Dad's computer to make more labels. This time they were for maths books; they said '*Always show your working!*' '*Practise your table facts*' and '*Use the chunking method*'.

'Nice, you've done a good job,' Amelia said. She looked sideways at Chloe. 'We've all done a good job. Mum's going to love it.'

Chloe's shoulders relaxed a bit and things went smoothly for the rest of the evening.

I was almost asleep when Chloe and Amelia came to bed. I heard Suvi whisper to them, 'Have you got everything you need packed up?'

'Yep,' Chloe said. 'Thanks so much for helping us today.'

'You're welcome.'

I heard the floorboards creak as she crept away and Amelia said, 'Suvi?'

'Yes?'

'Goodnight.'

I couldn't see in the dark, but I was pretty sure that Suvi was doing her smiley eyes.

It felt nicer in our bedroom than it had for a long time. I didn't worry about anything as I drifted off to sleep. It's amazing what a difference a tiny thing like a 'goodnight' can make.

CHAPTER ✤ TWENTY-FIVE

We raced home from school the next day and Amelia and I decorated while Chloe made fairy cakes. Lucy was at After School Club, but we promised to use the things she'd made the night before.

When we were little, we used to decorate each other's bedrooms with bead necklaces and bits of Christmas tinsel. The paper bunting looked much fancier, and Amelia had shown us how to make tissue-paper flowers and string them into a garland too. We looped that right across Mum's bedroom. It looked awesome.

Lucy had drawn a series of pictures, including one of all of us eating fairy cakes and one of the inspectors being blown up. We arranged them like a comic strip on the door. Then we went to help Chloe ice the cakes. They were still slightly warm from the oven, which made the icing a bit melty, but Chloe studded them with sugar roses and overall they looked really pretty.

When Mum's car drew up, we scrambled back up to her bedroom with our presents and the cakes on a cardboard cake stand. We heard Lucy first.

'Count to twenty then come upstairs,' she told Mum.

'This is very mysterious,' Mum said.

Lucy came thundering upstairs to join us. She looked up at the bunting and the flower garlands and mimed a 'Wow'.

I had to hold in a giggle while we listened to Mum coming up the stairs and along the landing. She tapped on the door.

'Come in!' said Lucy in such a serious, deep voice that my giggle escaped.

Mum pushed open the door and looked round at the pretty paper decorations and the parcels and the cakes on the bed.

'Oh, girls, it's a Whoopee!'

Her voice was a little bit wobbly.

Lucy held on to the end of the bed and jumped up and down. 'For you! Because you've been inspectored.'

'I can't think of anything more likely to cheer me up. What a lovely surprise! Who made these cakes?'

'I did,' Chloe said. 'Shall we eat some?'

'Let her open her presents first,' Amelia said.

So Mum opened her things. She put on her bracelet and she tucked my labels into her work bag straight away.

'They'll save me hours, Ella!' she said. 'That's a true gift.'

Amelia's present looked a bit small. It was just an envelope. Mum opened it and pulled out a letter. While she read it, her eyes were smiley like Suvi's, but full of tears too.

When she'd finished reading, she pulled Amelia into a hug.

'What was it?' Lucy asked. 'What did she give you?'

'I think it was a private letter,' Mum said.

Amelia was bright pink. She shrugged. 'I just said I'm sorry I've been such a whiney idiot and that I can see now that maybe moaning about Dad wasn't the best way to show my support for Mum, and that perhaps I could babysit for you pack of crazy monkeys some time.'

It sounded like she was going to try and carry on being not horrible. I thought that was a brilliant present.

'But you're supposed to make something!' Lucy said.

'She did make something,' Mum said. 'She made amends.'

'That means she's sorry,' Chloe explained to Lucy.

'Well, she could have done that ages ago,' Lucy said. 'Open mine!' she said to Mum. 'Mine's better than a sorry. Mine's got a whole roll of crêpe paper in it.'

Very gently, Mum opened Lucy's parcel. She smiled when she got to Lucy's creation.

'That is the most beautiful fl—'

'Bee swatter,' Lucy interrupted.

'Obviously,' Mum said. 'Quite clearly the most beautiful bee swatter I have ever seen. Thank you so much, girls.'

Chloe put on some music and Lucy acted out how to use the bee swatter again. Then Chloe imitated Lucy trying to persuade Madame Donna to wear a blindfold so that she can throw knives at her.

We laughed and laughed.

'Goodness, girls, you've really helped me forget all about those stupid inspectors,' Mum said.

'What were they like?' Lucy asked. 'Did they tell you you're rubbish?'

Amelia jabbed Lucy in the ribs. 'What?' Lucy asked. 'It was Mum that said she hadn't done enough work.'

Mum's face clouded. 'Lucy's right. I wasn't properly prepared for this. I kept putting things off, which I'm always telling you lot not to do. And then, when I did finally get down to it, I kept staying up too late and wearing myself out. I don't think I've set a very good example.'

Amelia had coloured up again. 'You kept putting off your work so you could do things with us and sort stuff out for us.'

'That's what I'm supposed to do. I'm your mum.'

'But we're not babies any more. We could do more to help you.' Amelia looked round at us. 'We can make our own packed lunches and do our own washing and ironing.'

Lucy's eyes lit up.

'I'll do Lucy's ironing,' Mum said firmly.

'We can keep on making the tea when you've got a meeting after school,' Chloe said.

'We could do it every night,' I said.

Mum smiled. 'Maybe a couple of nights a week.'

'And we could all do a better job of keeping the house tidy,' Amelia said. 'Instead of leaving it to Mum.' She looked at me. 'And Ella.'

I blushed. I hadn't realised that Amelia had noticed me helping Mum recently. It was nice to know she had.

'I can feed Buttercup,' Lucy said.

Mum ruffled her curls. 'Thank you, girls. And I'm going to make sure that I work hard when you're at your dad's and then I can enjoy spending time with you when you're at home without feeling guilty.'

'You know what else you should do sometimes when we're at Dad's?' Amelia said.

'What's that?'

'Go out with your friends and have fun.'

'I might just do that.' Mum pulled us all into one ginormous hug. 'You really are wonderful. And I'm sorry that things have been a bit chaotic around her for the last couple of weeks.'

'It hasn't been chaotic for the last couple of weeks,' Amelia said. 'It's more like the last few years.' But she said it in a smiling way.

'I like our house,' Chloe said. 'It's not chaotic, it's . . . full. Of our things and us and us doing stuff.'

'Well, that's not so bad then. But I am sorry that I'm such a stressed-out old badger.'

'You're not!' I said.

'Not all the time anyway,' Chloe said.

And that's true because, even though sometimes my mum goes mad because there are crumbs all over the sofa, sometimes she lets us lie on her bed and eat Whoopee fairy cakes with no plates at all.

CHAPTER ✿ TWENTY-SIX

'How's Thunder?' I asked Chloe. It was Sunday evening and we were washing up the tea things at Dad's house.

She stuck a finger in the custard jug and licked it. 'Better. I had a talk like you suggested.'

'What did you say?'

'I said, "Are you being funny with me because I said I didn't want to go to the disco with you?"'

That wasn't exactly the sort of thing that I imagined her saying when I told her to talk to him. 'What did he say?'

'He just mumbled and went bright red. So I told him it wasn't because I didn't like him. I mean, he's not very good-looking, but he is quite good at football and he's excellent at fitting things in his mouth.'

'Did you tell him that stuff?'

'Yeah.'

'And did that cheer him up?'

'Seemed to, which is pretty dumb really because obviously I like him and obviously we have fun together.'

'Do you know what, Clo? I think that you're the sort of person who knows things without people having to say them, but some people need help seeing stuff clearly. You have to tell them how you feel.'

'Yeah, that's definitely true about Thunder.'

'I'm like that too.'

She nodded. 'I think, even though she's all prickly, that's really what Amelia is like too.'

We thought about that for a minute. I knew Chloe was right. The last couple of weeks had shown that Amelia wasn't the tough girl we'd thought she was.

'Anyway, thanks for helping me with Thunder; we're definitely good friends again now.'

Dad came into the kitchen while Chloe was talking.

'Thunder?' he said. 'Is he a new friend?'

Chloe squirted more washing-up liquid into the already bubbly water. 'He's not exactly new any more.'

'Oh. And what about you, Ella? Who's your best buddy at the moment?'

'Kayleigh of course and Ashandra next door, remember?'

Dad crossed his eyes. 'I can hardly keep up.'

He was trying to be funny, but for some reason it made me mad. Really mad.

'That's because you don't try! You don't know anything that anybody is doing because you're never here and when you are you don't listen to us.'

My words hit him in the face like gravel.

He blinked a bit. 'Well, I know I've been busy lately.'

'You're always busy!'

'Ella, listen, I—'

'No, you listen. You told me that you were looking forward to watching Kirsti grow up, but you're already missing her doing cute stuff because you're working late. And it's not just about Kirsti; you've got us as well. We haven't finished growing up; you should be enjoying us too!'

I stumbled towards the door. Chloe put a hand on my arm, but I shook her off. 'I'm going to Ashandra's,' I said. And I went out before either of them could stop me. I even slammed the door.

I didn't actually go straight to Ashandra's because

I was too upset. I walked all the way down to the roundabout in a rage. It took me a while to calm down enough to go back and ring on Ashandra's doorbell.

She opened the door herself. 'Hey,' she said. 'I was just going to call for you. I wanted to talk to you about something.'

She took me up to her room. Ash's bedroom is like a library; one wall is covered in shelves full of books and in front of the books she puts interesting stuff like the fossils her dad takes her hunting for or the little figures that you get in *Kinder* Eggs. She's even got a tiny family of dolls sitting there. Ash would never hide anything she liked under her bed.

'Are you OK?' she asked. 'You look a bit funny.'

'I had a row with my dad.'

She raised her eyebrows. 'Really? You never row with people; at least, normally you never do.'

'I'm cross with him. He doesn't listen to me.'

She put an arm round me. 'Do you want to talk about it?'

I shook my head. I knew that if I talked about it I'd cry.

'Do you want a Coke and some cookies?'

I nodded.

Ashandra brought them upstairs and then we played on her computer. She talked about cheerful things instead and I was glad she did.

'Kayleigh showed me this really good website where you can learn all the different kinds of horse tack,' she said.

'That's good.'

She took a deep breath. 'I wanted to apologise to you, Ella. I shouldn't have been so rude about Kayleigh to you.'

She was watching me very closely so I gave her a little nod.

'I mean, you know what I'm like. I want things to be perfect and I can be a bit stroppy, especially when other people are more laid-back. Obviously, Kayleigh doesn't know that and she probably just thought I was evil.'

I laughed. 'You were both a bit hard on each other.'

'I know. Kayleigh says that she was worried that everyone at secondary school would be better at stuff than her and that they'd make her feel like an idiot, so when I started bossing her about she got really angry.'

That made sense. Kayleigh is definitely more likely to shout than to cry when she's upset, but I was surprised to think of Ash and Kay getting stressed about school. And also a bit shocked that they didn't tell me about it.

'It's understandable really,' Ash said.

I smoothed out her pillow. 'How come you two suddenly started understanding each other?'

I thought that she was going to say that my tough attitude forced them to take a good look at things, but instead she said, 'We were worried about you.'

'Were you?'

'Yeah, you didn't seem like yourself. We started talking about if you were OK in maths and we thought that maybe we'd upset you so we came up with the idea of going riding to cheer you up.'

I nearly laughed. Sitting on top of one of those giant stompers is not my idea of being cheered up.

'But then we talked a bit more and . . . I think she's nice.'

'She is. So are you. That's what I kept telling you two.'

'Maybe we just needed to work it out for ourselves.'

I smiled.

'But I feel really bad that you got in the middle of it all. I'm sorry I was all bossy and rude. I feel even worse now that I know you're having problems with your dad.'

I sniffed.

'Do you want to talk about it now? If you don't, we could watch a DVD, but we can, you know, if you want.'

It all came pouring out. How he's always late home from work, even on Wednesdays when he's supposed to be seeing us, and how even though he makes Plans for the weekend half the time he's still thinking about work. And how it's hard to get him to listen to me because when he does pay anyone any attention he's talking sports with Chloe or cooing over Kirsti.

'That's horrible,' Ashandra said. 'I'm glad you shouted at him.'

I scrunched a handful of duvet. 'I'm not sure it was a very good idea. I've calmed down now and I feel a bit bad.'

'Don't feel bad: he deserved it. But maybe you could talk to him? My mum's always really busy with work, but we had a chat about it last year and now we always spend Saturday afternoon together. Maybe you could have a special afternoon with your dad?'

But I knew there was no way Dad could squeeze a special afternoon with each of his daughters into a week.

When I got back from Ashandra's, I went straight to bed. I should have been happy that Ash and Kay were finally getting on, but I was still upset about Dad. I felt horrible about shouting at him. It was a stupid idea to try to be tough. I couldn't pretend not to care about things because I did. I cared a lot. It had even turned out that Amelia cared about things too. She was only horrible because she was upset about Mum and Dad splitting up.

I'd thought that being tough had got Ashandra and Kayleigh to talk to each other, but now Ashandra had told me that they'd started talking because they were worried about me. They went riding because they wanted to make me happy. They were being nice. So maybe being nice was the right thing after all.

I hadn't got very far trying to be like Amelia or by following Chloe's lead. And there was no way I could ever hope to be like Lucy. You're either born a Lucy or you're not.

Maybe Mum was right in the first place and I should be myself.

In the morning, Dad left for work before I got up. I was glad to go to school to have something else to think about and because I was looking forward to hanging out with Ashandra and Kayleigh now that they were friends and I wasn't pretending to be hard any more. Except that, when we got to school, all that Ashandra and Kayleigh seemed to talk about was the art competition and horses. So I ended up having to pretend not to care about things after all.

CHAPTER ✦ TWENTY–SEVEN

Tuesday was International Day. I was excited about doing lots of activities instead of normal lessons, but I was glad that they gave us a timetable so I knew exactly where I had to be at what time.

Before break, we did African dancing. I was a bit self-conscious, but I liked it when it was my group's turn to play the drums while the others danced. After break, we had half-an-hour taster sessions of different activities. Our tutor group did yodelling, International Sign Language and capoeira.

At lunchtime, we could buy the Year Nine's cooking from around the world. I bought three mini samosas from Amelia to share with Ashandra and Kayleigh. When I brought them back to the table, they were talking about the art competition.

Again. It was nice to see them getting excited about it, but I was still feeling horrible about shouting at Dad and I wished they'd talk to me and take my mind off it.

After lunch, everyone was herded into the sports hall, which was the only place big enough to fit the whole school plus lots of parents. All around the edges were the competition panels. Year Sevens were let into the hall first so while we were waiting for everybody else to file in we swivelled our necks about to check out the other classes' panels.

'Some of them are really good,' Ashandra said.

'That's Chloe's class's,' I said, pointing to the Finland panel, but Ash and Kay were discussing our chances with their heads bent together. I looked back to Chloe's class's panel; they'd done a good job. When you looked closely, you could see that there was a tiny army of Moomins marching round the outside edge. Some other Year Eights had done the USA, using loads of little pictures to make up a big image of the stars and stripes flag. It was really effective. I still thought ours was the best, but my nana always said not to count your chickens before they hatch, so I tried not to get my hopes up about a prize. Even so, I definitely saw a lot of people admiring the dragon bursting out of the background. The tiny lights in the lanterns really grabbed your attention too.

Ashandra and Kayleigh hadn't even noticed that I wasn't joining in with their conversation. They'd moved on to discussing their waiter at Pizza Hut and his crazy hairstyle. Somehow, that wound back to horse riding.

'Are we still on for Wednesday in half-term?' Ashandra asked.

'Definitely,' Kayleigh said, smiling.

I didn't say anything because I didn't know about Wednesday in half-term and I was pretty sure that that meant I wasn't invited.

'We're going riding,' Ashandra explained to me. Then, seeing the look on my face, she quickly added, 'You didn't want to come, did you?'

I'd spent enough time talking to Suvi now to know that it's not a good idea to do something that you don't like just to please other people. Especially when it seemed like they wouldn't even be that thrilled to have you there anyway.

'No,' I said. 'I don't think riding is really my thing.'

'That's what we thought,' Kayleigh said.

Which should have been fine. It should have been brilliant that finally they were getting along. But somehow I didn't feel too good. So far, them getting on didn't seem to mean we were doing things together: it meant I was feeling left out.

Our head teacher got up on a temporary platform made out of those big stage blocks and the hall fell silent. First, she said how delighted she was to see so many parents and then she told us how lucky we were to have enjoyed such a great range of activities. After that, we watched displays of some of the different activities: morris dancing, tae kwon do and gamelan music. I was glad our tutor group hadn't been chosen to display anything.

To finish it all off we had three different songs from the Year Nines. Amelia's was last. When she got up on the stage, my heart started beating really hard. I hoped that her voice wouldn't crack and she wouldn't drop the microphone. It was the song that she had written. Chloe was right: it was all about harmony between countries; they must have been told to make it about that stuff because usually Amelia prefers to sing about things dying, but it was really good. Amelia sang the verses and the rest of her class joined in with the chorus. You could see people in the audience swaying; it was an excellent song. They got a very big cheer at the end. I saw Amelia's eyes catch on someone and when I turned to see who it was I spotted my dad in the second row of parents. He was standing up and clapping. He's got a very loud cheer.

He'd come! Surely Amelia would forgive him now? I hoped he'd forgiven me for shouting at him.

Finally, the head got to the art competition; she rambled on a bit, but I hardly heard that part.

'In third place we have 8NM with Finland.'

A giant whoop went up behind us. I didn't need to turn round to know that it was Chloe.

'In second place . . .'

I turned to look at Ashandra and Kayleigh; they were gripping each other's hands tight.

'. . . 8RP with Spain.'

More shouting and clapping. Either we'd won or we hadn't come anywhere at all. I touched Ash's arm, but she didn't notice.

'And the winners are . . . 7CE with their striking representation of China.'

We'd won! All around me, our whole class were squealing and cheering. I turned to Ash and Kay. They were locked in a fierce hug.

'We're the winners!' Alenka said to me and she held up her hand for a high five.

'It's brilliant,' I said, smacking her hand.

But actually I didn't feel very brilliantish.

The head did a bit more telling us how talented

and lucky we all were and then it was time to go home.

Dad was waiting for us at the gates.

Chloe beamed when she saw him. 'Did you see my panel? What did you think of the midnight sun? I did that.'

I thought that Amelia might run into Dad's arms when she saw him, like they do in films. She didn't. Instead, she said, 'Hi,' like people do in real life. It wasn't even a very excited 'hi'.

Dad took us to the café over the road to have cakes. Amelia waited till he'd brought the tray over and sat down.

'You can't just sort everything out by managing to turn up for once in your life,' she told him.

I put down my cake. I didn't want to hear any more fighting.

But Dad didn't shout; he just nodded.

'That would be like me expecting you to forget about me being rude to you and Suvi for over a year just because I said sorry,' Amelia said, staring at her hands.

'Amelia, I am going to forget about that because I understand that you've been angry. And you don't have to forgive me, although it would make me very happy if you did.'

Amelia didn't say anything.

Dad took a deep breath. 'I've spoken to your mother and it's become abundantly clear that I should have done more to help you all adjust to how things have changed. I'm really, really sorry that I've let you all down.'

He looked at me. It seemed like he really was sorry.

Amelia still didn't answer.

'I want you to know that it doesn't matter how mad you get at me. I will always be your dad and I will always love you.'

He didn't mind that I'd said those mean things. I let out a long breath. I felt better than I had done all day.

But Amelia wasn't convinced. 'If you love us so much, why do you spend so much time at work?'

Dad rubbed at his forehead. 'I know it doesn't make any sense to you, but I work so hard because of you, because of my family.'

'Do you mean money?' Chloe asked. 'Because presents and stuff are cool, but we like it when you're home.'

'I know that and we have time together most weekends, don't we?'

Maybe he really didn't realise how much time he was spending in his study or that when he was with us it wasn't doing things we wanted to do.

Amelia raised her eyebrows.

'Well, perhaps not enough.' Dad fiddled with a teaspoon. 'I just want to make sure you've all got security.'

I remember what Mum said. 'Is it something to do with when you were younger?' I asked.

Dad sighed. 'Yes, yes, I guess that's where this all started. When I was your age, Ella, my dad lost his job. For a long time after that, we didn't have any money for luxuries; sometimes we didn't even have the money for basics.'

I didn't know that. I knew that my dad's family weren't very well off and sometimes he said, 'When I was a boy, we never had any of this,' but I hadn't realised that they were properly poor.

'That's sad,' Chloe said.

'It was tough, but it made me very determined. I knew that I was going to work hard at school and that I was going to do well so that I could give my family anything they wanted.'

Amelia looked right into Dad's eyes. 'We want you.'

Dad blinked. 'I've been a bit of an idiot, haven't I? It's taken me a long time, too long, to realise what you really need, but from now on I'm going to be here for you. All of you.'

'Really?' Amelia asked, not in a bored, sarcastic,

I-don't-believe-you way, but in a hopeful, wanting way.

'I'm going to make some changes. No more overtime. And no more pushing my hobbies on you all.'

Chloe threw her arms round Dad.

Amelia just said, 'Good.'

But I think she meant it as much as the hug.

CHAPTER ❤ TWENTY-EIGHT

Dad drove us home.

'How did you even know I was singing?' Amelia asked.

'Chloe told me.'

'Chloe?' Amelia swivelled round in her seat to look at Chloe, but she had her earphones plugged in and was digging about in the bottom of her bag for loose Skittles.

'Yes,' Dad said. 'Not only did she tell me that you were singing a solo, she also said that if I didn't come and watch you she would put Buttercup's droppings in my muesli.'

I was sitting right behind Amelia so I couldn't guess what she thought about that by the back of her head, but I could tell she was thinking.

I was so happy that Amelia had made up with

Dad and that he seemed to have forgiven me, and that Ashandra and Kayleigh were getting on better than they had done all term. But somehow my insides felt grindy and I had to go and lie on my bed to try and think of bright sides, but my head was too scrambly so I just lay with my eyes closed instead.

After a while, I heard Mum and Lucy come in. Chloe and Amelia were talking loudly and I guessed they were telling her about this afternoon. Then I heard Mum's footsteps coming up the stairs and into my room. I don't have to think of bright sides about my mum. That's how good she is. One of her best good bits is that she knows how you're feeling. Sometimes she even knows how you're feeling before you do.

She came and sat on my bed.

'Did you hear about Dad and Amelia?' I asked.

She nodded. 'I'm glad they've worked things out. And I hear he's going to stop working so much when he's at home. That means you'll see more of him.'

I nodded a bit.

'How was International Day?' she asked.

'We won the art competition.'

'That's brilliant! Ashandra and Kayleigh must have been really pleased. Are they still getting on?'

216

'Yep. Really well. They hugged a lot when we won. It's really good.'

She put a cool hand on my forehead. 'Are you all playing together?'

I didn't explain to Mum that you're not supposed to do playing at secondary school.

'They're going riding together at half-term.'

'You're not so keen on riding, are you?'

I shook my head.

'Do you mind if they go without you?'

'Not really.'

'But . . .?'

'I don't mind them going riding because I don't really want to do that, but they have been talking about horses a lot and they sit together in maths and they went out for pizza and they're both really nice so obviously they would like each other, and I wanted them to get on so much, so I should feel happy . . . But I feel a tiny bit left out.'

Mum smoothed my hair back off my face. 'I can understand that. When there are three people, sometimes it's hard to work out how you fit together.'

'I do want them to be friends.'

'I know. And I think they probably don't realise that you're feeling left out. Why don't you tell Kayleigh and Ashandra?'

217

'They might be cross. And it might start an argument.'

'I don't think they'd be cross.'

'They would. They'd say, "Don't you want us to be friends?" and "You're the one who said we should spend time together." And then there'd be a big argument.'

She was watching me. 'And you wouldn't like that?'

'Nobody likes arguments. Except Lucy. And she only likes them when she wins them. Or if someone else is having them and she gets to watch one of the someones bash the other someone over the head.'

'Arguments can be horrible, but once people have said what they think then hopefully it can all be sorted out.'

I pushed myself into a sitting position. 'That's not what happens in an argument!'

'No?'

'No. People get upset. Very upset and things are broken and in the end it all finishes and you're not friends any more.'

'I think that's a bit drastic.'

'That's what happened with you and Dad.'

Mum's pulled her head back in surprise. 'Ella . . . It's important to tell people how you feel. Talking about your feelings doesn't have to lead to an argument and, even if it does, an argument doesn't mean the end of a friendship.'

'But you and Dad . . .'

'Dad and I stopped getting along. Stopped enjoying spending time together. Stopped wanting the same things. That's why we're not married any more. At the time, when things were going wrong, the best thing we did was talk to each other about how we felt. Because it helped us understand each other. I think it would be much harder for a relationship to end without understanding why.'

'But I don't want things to end with Kayleigh and Ashandra.'

'Getting divorced was the answer that Dad and I got to. You and Kayleigh and Ashandra aren't me and your father.'

'Maybe I'm just being selfish.'

'Do you want them to stop riding together?'

'No, I don't mind that.'

'But you'd rather that they didn't talk horses non-stop when they're with you?'

'Yes.'

'That's not selfish; that's a completely reasonable request.'

'I suppose so.'

'You can't go on pretending not to be unhappy.

It'll make you even more unhappy. You'll be so unhappy that you'll burst. I'll get covered in Ella gloop.'

I almost managed a laugh. 'I guess I could talk to them.'

'I think that's a really good idea.'

She slipped an arm round me. 'I'm wondering if Ashandra and Kayleigh aren't the only ones that you've been trying really hard to please.'

'What do you mean?'

'Dad told Amelia that he'd love her no matter what, didn't he?'

'Yes.'

'That goes for you too. You don't have to do anything special; you don't have to be the good one or the nice one; he'll love you anyway. And if you talk to him about your feelings he's not going to go away.'

I didn't know what to say to that.

She squeezed me. 'I hid the last of the fairy cakes in the washing machine. Do you want one?'

I followed her downstairs. My mum is magic. Not only does she know exactly what I'm thinking, she's also smart enough to think of the only place in the house that Chloe would never dream of looking for cake.

*

Amelia surprised everybody by making dinner. It was a proper one with vegetables and everything. When Lucy came out of the Pit and upstairs to the table, she wouldn't eat anything until someone else had tried it, but everything actually tasted really good.

When Amelia leant over the table to pass me the potatoes, I saw something on her arms. So did Chloe. She wasn't wearing her usual black wristbands; she was wearing seven bead bracelets. Every Whoopee bracelet that Chloe had ever made her.

Chloe's mouth was open.

Amelia realised that she'd noticed them and her cheeks started to flush.

'You kept them,' Chloe said.

Mum looked up.

'Of course I kept them,' Amelia said.

Lucy speared a carrot with her knife. 'She keeps them in a special box.'

Everybody turned to look at her. I hoped we weren't going to get into an argument about Lucy going into Amelia's room.

'What?' Lucy said. 'She does.'

Chloe was still staring at Amelia. 'I thought you hated me.'

Amelia took a deep breath. 'I don't hate you. I

221

don't hate anyone. I've been a bit . . . confused. I was really mad at Dad and I got mad at you too because I thought you were siding with him.'

'I wasn't.'

'I know and I'm sorry.'

'That's OK. I didn't really get it before, I didn't realise how upset you were or that you needed to talk about stuff. I probably should have been a bit more, you know . . . *sensitive* about your feelings.'

She pulled such a revolted face when she said 'sensitive' that we all laughed.

Lucy pointed her speared carrot at Amelia. 'So were you just saying all that mean stuff to us because you wanted to live with Dad and Kirsti?' she asked.

Amelia shrugged. 'Not exactly. I was angry at him for leaving, but I suppose I understand it a bit more now.'

'But will you stop being an idiot?' Chloe asked.

'Takes one to know one,' Amelia said and she flicked a piece of broccoli at Chloe.

I took that as a yes.

CHAPTER ✿TWENTY-NINE

Sometimes you listen to people tell you stuff and you don't really believe them, but once it's in your head your brain thinks about it even when you don't know it's doing it and eventually it starts to make sense. I *had* been trying to make Dad happy. I had been trying to get him to like me by being the nice one, and then I tried to join in with stuff that he likes, and then I tried not to care if he upset me. And I'd already worked out that pretending to be something you're not is a bad idea with your friends so it was pretty obvious that it wasn't a good idea with my own dad either.

I definitely needed to tell Dad how I felt.

On the way back from school, I wondered how I was going to bring it up. Dad was home when we got in and the first thing he said was, 'Ella, can I talk to you?'

My stomach swooped. This was my opportunity.

He led me out into the garden and brushed the leaves off one of the metal garden chairs for me to sit on. 'I wanted to apologise,' he said.

'I wanted to say sorry too!'

'What on earth for?'

I gripped my chair. 'For being horrible. Saying that stuff about you not knowing anything about me.'

Dad shook his head. 'You weren't horrible at all, Ella. I think there was a lot of truth in what you said.'

I remembered what I said to Chloe about telling people how you feel. I pulled at a thread on my hem. 'I would like to talk to you more.'

Dad nodded. 'There are a lot of voices in this family and I shouldn't let you get shouted down by the others.'

Even though it was chilly in the garden in just my cardie, I could feel my face getting hot. 'I feel a bit stupid saying all this,' I said.

'I don't think you're the stupid one. I think I've been stupid not to make sure that you know that I really want to hear what you've got to say.'

'I probably should have been more like Chloe an—'

'No.' He gripped my hand. 'Absolutely not. I want you to be exactly as you are.'

'But I'm not very good at some things.'

'To me you're absolutely perfect. I don't want you to change anything.'

'But if I was like Amel—'

'Amelia is perfect as Amelia and you are perfectly Ella. I love you just the way you are.'

Then I felt warm all over. But in a good way.

Dad put an arm round me. 'I've got something to show you all, but I'd like you to see it first.'

'What is it?'

He unlocked the door that goes from the garden into the garage and pointed into the gloom.

I stepped inside. It was a new car. A big new car. One of those ones with an extra row of seats.

'See?' Dad said. 'It's a seven-seater. That way no one will get left behind.'

I couldn't believe it.

'Wasn't it really expensive?' I asked.

'Ella, I would spend all the money in the world to show you that there is always room for you.'

Dad let me try all the different seats and all the buttons. And we talked. I told him about Kayleigh and Ashandra and riding and the art competition and about Chloe and Amelia being friends again and that I got a hundred per cent in my maths test last week.

It was a really good chat.

*

I was so happy about how well it went with Dad that I didn't find it nearly as difficult as I thought I would to grab Ashandra and Kayleigh after maths the next day and say, 'Can I talk to you two about something?'

'Of course,' Ashandra said and Kay nodded her head.

Which surprised me because, when I'd been thinking about this conversation in my head, I had imagined them saying, 'Sorry, we've got to chat about fetlocks and those knotty horse hairstyles and we haven't really got time to listen to you,' which just goes to show that Chloe is right and my imagination makes up far worse stuff than what is actually happening in real life.

'Shall we sit under the tree?' I asked.

'OK,' Ashandra said.

'Is this something really serious?' Kayleigh asked. 'Are you breaking up with us?'

'Don't be silly,' Ashandra said. Then she looked at me. 'You're not breaking up with us, are you?'

'Of course not. I always want to be friends with you. Although it was quite hard for me when you two didn't get on.'

'Sorry,' Ashandra said. 'I don't think we realised how much you minded until you went all funny and angry.'

'I really like you both and I wanted us all to get on.'

'I know,' Kayleigh said. 'But you did keep trying to squish us together and at first . . .' She looked at Ashandra.

'At first, you couldn't stand me!'

They burst out laughing.

'I know and you didn't like me,' said Kayleigh.

Ashandra pretended to bash her on the head. 'I thought you didn't care about anything. But I know you do now. Anyway, you thought I was posh!'

'You are a bit posh.'

Ashandra stuck her nose in the air and crossed her eyes.

Kayleigh gave her a push. 'But you're really nice as well.'

'I'm really happy you two like each other,' I said. 'It's just that recently you only seem to talk about the art competition, your pizza waiter or horses and I feel a bit left out.'

'Oh,' Kayleigh said. 'We didn't know. I'm really sorry.'

Ashandra put an arm round me. 'So am I. We won't talk about horses ever again.'

'No! You can talk about horses. Just . . . maybe not all the time.'

Kayleigh nodded. 'OK. Cool.'

The knot in my stomach loosened. 'This is excellent, now we can all be definitely best friends forever.' I smiled.

Ashandra and Kayleigh exchanged a look.

'What?' I asked.

'Listen, Ella, we both think you're brilliant and Kayleigh and I are definitely going to go riding together and keep sitting together in maths, even if Mr Garibaldi says we don't have to, but . . .'

'You and me are already best friends, aren't we?' Kayleigh asked. 'And Ash and Erica like a lot of the same things – like reading massive piles of books and being completely brainy and they're sort of best friends now, aren't you, Ash?'

Ashandra nodded.

'Oh.' Now that I thought about it, Ash and Erica had been spending a lot of time together, but I suppose I'd been too focused on being nice or sporty or tough to really notice.

'Is that OK?' Ash asked.

I thought about it. It wasn't my plan, but you can't always know where things are going to end up. You can't always map out what people mean to you. Kayleigh is my best friend, Ash is my best friend at my dad's, Ash and Kay are good friends and Erica seems nice so maybe we could be friends too. They're not all exactly the same kind of friendship, but they're all good. And that's what matters.

'Yes,' I said. 'That's completely fine.'

'Good,' said Ashandra. And then she poked Kayleigh. 'If you call me posh again, I'll push you in the swimming pool.'

When I got home, I told Mum about Ashandra and Kayleigh. I also told her about Erica and Alenka and some of the other people in my class.

'It sounds like you've got lots of different friends, Ella. I knew you would have; you're a very special girl.'

I smiled.

'I've got an idea. Would you like to have a sleepover in half-term?'

'That's a brilliant idea.'

'Who will you ask? Ash and Kay and Alenka and Erica?'

I thought about it. 'Can I invite everyone?'

'Everyone?'

'Well, all the girls in my tutor group. There are thirteen including me. I don't want to leave anybody out.'

'Of course you can. You'd better make some invitations.'

CHAPTER 🍓 THIRTY

Three days before my party, Amelia actually said that she'd help me make flower garlands to decorate. We spread out over the kitchen table and Chloe came in to see what we were doing.

'Do you want some help? I could make a garland of monkey butts.'

'Yes to the help, no to the monkey backsides,' I said.

She sat down. 'Are you having this party in the Pit?' she asked.

'I suppose so.'

'How many people are coming?' Amelia asked.

I looked down at my flower. 'I invited twelve . . .'

'Really? You invited everyone?' Amelia frowned. 'Even that horrible Jasmine girl you've been moaning about?'

'I couldn't help it. I don't want to be the sort of person that leaves people out. Even if that does mean they laugh at me when I give them an invitation.'

'So you're not really expecting Jasmine to turn up?'

'Actually, the only people who have definitely said yes are Ash, Kay, Alenka and Erica.'

'Oh,' Chloe said. 'Well, it was quite short notice.' She drew a monkey bottom on a piece of paper. 'And five people is loads for a sleepover.'

'But you do still need the Pit really,' Amelia said. 'Has Lucy finished whatever she's doing in there?'

'The tape's still up.'

'You'll just have to ask her to take it down when she comes back from Dad's.'

Lucy had convinced Dad to let her stay an extra day after our weekend with him.

'She's probably reading Kirsti her Victorians project for the millionth time,' Chloe said.

'Lucky Kirsti,' Amelia said. She hadn't completely given up on the sarcasm.

Mum's phone rang inside her bag in the hall. I stood up, but Mum came out of the sitting room and grabbed it so I went back to the garlands.

'Oh my God,' Mum said.

We stopped threading flowers and started listening.

'But didn't you see? Weren't you watching them?' Mum asked.

I looked at Amelia then Chloe. Something bad was happening.

'Have you phoned the police?' Mum's voice was strange and tight. 'What did they say? Yes, I'll come now. Ring me again if you find them.'

'What is it?' Amelia asked as soon as Mum hung up.

'It's Lucy and Kirsti.'

My insides squeezed hard.

'They're missing.'

'How can they be missing?' Chloe asked. 'They're at Dad's house.'

'He says Suvi was having a shower while Kirsti was sleeping, and Lucy was reading next to her basket, and he left them alone just for a moment so he could start tea and then the next time he looked they'd gone, both of them.'

'But how?' Chloe's hands gripped the edge of the table.

'He says . . .' Mum's chin shook. 'He's says the window was open . . .'

Amelia very gently steered Mum into a chair.

My mind was in overdrive thinking of horrible things that could have happened.

'Are the police looking for them?' Chloe asked.

'The police are on their way to Dad's. I need to

go . . .' She stood up and looked around as if she couldn't remember where the door was.

'What should we do?' Chloe asked.

'I . . .' Mum's face was white.

My heart was thumping. What if something really bad had happened? But Lucy would scream if anyone tried to take Kirsti; she would never let anything happen to her, she loves her so much. Then it hit me.

'It was Lucy,' I said.

They all looked at me.

'You know she's crazy about Kirsti. I bet she took her. Maybe she went for a walk with her.'

'She's not allowed out by herself, she knows that!' Mum said.

'When Lucy knows things, she doesn't always do them,' Chloe pointed out.

Amelia had picked up her phone and hit some buttons.

'Dad?' she said into it. 'Yes, I know. No, we haven't found her. Listen, is the pram gone? Did Lucy take the pram?'

That was a very clever thing to think of.

'He's looking,' Amelia said to us. We waited. Amelia's face lit up. 'It's gone! That's good. Lucy's taken Kirsti out, but we can find them. Yes, we'll go now.'

She hung up.

'Mum, you go in the car.' She handed her her phone and her keys. 'Chloe and I will go to the shop and the swings. Ella, stay here in case they come back.'

'Check your room,' Mum said to me. 'See if she's taken anything. Or left a note.'

I ran up the stairs and looked on Lucy's bed and around the room, but I couldn't find anything helpful.

So Mum dashed off to Dad's house and Chloe and Amelia left to search too. I sat next to the phone in case Lucy called. But I knew she wouldn't. She hadn't got a phone and I didn't think she would even be tall enough to reach the slot to put the money in a phone box. Besides, I was pretty sure that she didn't want anyone to know where she was because she wanted to be alone with Kirsti. I felt sick in my stomach. Lucy is smart, but what if she forgot to look both ways when she crossed the road?

I should have known that something like this was going to happen. I could see how miserable she was about Kirsti. I should have tried harder to make Dad and Mum understand that Lucy was horribly upset about not living with Kirsti. I really thought that I had helped by telling Lucy that she could teach Kirsti everything about being a Strawberry Sister. The day before, at Dad's, I'd heard Lucy singing Kirsti the rude song that Chloe made up about farting in the bath. She seemed so cheerful that I was sure I'd solved her problem. But perhaps I should never have said that stuff about teaching Kirsti because maybe that's what gave Lucy the idea that it was OK to go wandering off with her. I wish I'd been better at helping. If anything happened to either of them, it would be all my fault.

I lifted the phone up to check that it was working, then put it back down again quickly just in case that was the exact moment that Lucy chose to call. I went to the window to see if she was coming down the road, but she wasn't. I filled a glass of water from the tap, but it was hard to swallow so I poured it away again. I stared around at the untidy kitchen and decided to get started on the washing-up, but all the time I couldn't stop thinking about Lucy and Kirsti. Kirsti still needed feeding all the time. Suvi said baby stomachs are weeny so, even when she's just had a feed, it's not long before Kirsti is starving again. What if she was crying now?

My mind felt like it was doing crazy loop-the-loops. I needed to think straight. I sat down on the sofa and took ten deep breaths.

If Lucy really was trying to show Kirsti how to be a Strawberry Sister, where would she take her? Lucy loves the fountain and the milkshake shop, but they're both in the town centre. Surely she wouldn't go that far? There's the swings and the newsagent's where we buy sweets, but Amelia and Chloe were going to check them. I tried to remember exactly what Lucy said when she told me that she thought Kirsti was missing out. She was talking about March of the Zombies while she was swinging from her bat bar . . . Her bat bar! Maybe that's where she was.

I grabbed my phone and my key from the table in the hall and sped out of the door.

As I hurried across the road, I was completely convinced that I'd find Lucy showing her bat bar to Kirsti.

I slipped through the gate. The skate ramp was blocking my view of the bat bar. My strides turned to a run. I stopped dead.

They weren't there.

CHAPTER ❤ THIRTY-ONE

My shoulders sagged. Lucy could be anywhere. Poor Kirsti would be howling. What if they were lost? What if a creepy stranger kidnapped them?

'Ella?'

I swung round. It was Lucy. With Kirsti in her pram.

My knees wobbled. 'Lucy! Where have you been? Everyone is looking for you and Kirsti. Is she OK?' I looked into the pram. Kirsti was fast asleep with a smile on her face.

'She's fine. She hasn't even listened to what I've been telling her. She's just been napping.'

'Lucy, the police are looking for you!'

'Why? Didn't Dad read my note?'

'What note? Nobody said anything about a note.'

Lucy rolled her eyes in exasperation. 'I wrote a note telling him to come to our house.'

'Why? Never mind. Come on, we've got to go home.'

I pulled up Mum's number from my contacts and called her.

Mum answered straight away. 'Have you found them?'

'Yes, it's OK, they're OK. They were by the skate ramp.'

Mum made a gaspy sound. 'Oh my goodness. Stay where you are. No, wait, take them home, take them straight home. Don't stop for anything. I was on my way to check Rose's house. I'm very close. I'll be there in three minutes.'

'OK.'

'Take them back to the house now. Promise me, Ella? Straight back to the house.'

'I promise.'

We had only just managed to wrestle the pram in through the door when Mum's car pulled up. She burst in through the door with Chloe and Amelia right behind her. Mum pushed past me and for a moment I thought she was going to shake Lucy, but then she wrapped her arms round her.

'Don't ever, ever do that again,' she said. Very gently, she lifted Kirsti out of her pram. 'Is she all right?'

'She's fine,' Lucy said. 'Why are you fussing?'

'Lucy Jane Strawberry!' Mum said in a very loud whisper so as not to startle Kirsti. 'Don't pretend you don't know that what you have just done was both remarkably stupid and extremely dangerous! You're not old enough to be out by yourself and you are certainly not old enough to be in charge of a tiny baby.'

Lucy's face crumpled.

'I just wanted Kirsti to come here!'

Mum handed Kirsti to Amelia and gripped Lucy by the shoulders. 'Lucy, look at me. You must never go out by yourself again. Promise me.'

Mum was so serious and quiet-voiced that Lucy was already hiccuping with tears.

'I promise,' she said.

'Good.' She pulled Lucy into another hug. 'You've scared us silly. Poor Suvi is beside herself. They'll be here in a few minutes and you must say how awfully sorry you are.'

'Will they take Kirsti back?' Lucy asked in a very quiet, un-Lucyish voice.

Mum's eyes widened. 'Of course they will!'

Lucy's chin sank to her chest.

'You must have known that would happen,' Mum said.

'But I thought . . . I thought that if I got Kirsti home then we could all live here.'

We looked at each other. Lucy was still hoping for one big family house.

'I don't think Suvi could live here,' I said. 'She doesn't like big messes; she'd go insane just looking at Book Mountain.'

'I know that,' Lucy said. 'That's why I made them something. Look, I'll show you.' She turned and went down the stairs to the basement. Mum followed, with her eyebrows up in her hair, and the rest of us trailed behind her. Lucy tore the tape off the door to the Pit and pushed it open.

Inside was transformed. All the toys and junk had disappeared. The floor had been scrubbed and Lucy's mural had been painted over (one wall was white and one was lilac: I recognised the paint from the shed). The toy cars and the train track and the dolls' heads and the leaky felt tips and the piles of Lego were all gone. Everything was very neat and very tidy. The sofa was covered with clean white bedding and Amelia's old doll's cot was made up in the corner. I sucked in my breath. Lucy had made a bedroom and it wasn't hard to guess who for.

I looked at Lucy. Her red–gold fringe was stuck

to her forehead with jam. There was a tomato-sauce stain on her T-shirt. Her elbows were scabbed and there was a streak of dirt across her cheek. Lucy had never made anything neat or tidy in her life. She hated neat and tidy. She hated cleaning up. When she saw white things, her fingers itched to cover them with blobs of colour. But she had made this room. This was how much she wanted Kirsti and Dad and Suvi to live with us. I reached out and held Lucy's hand.

'Oh, Lucy,' Mum said. 'What a lovely thing to do! But Dad and Suvi have got their own house with their things in; they can't squeeze in here.'

Lucy's face crumpled.

The doorbell rang.

'That will be Dad,' Amelia said.

We followed Mum, carrying Kirsti, back upstairs. She opened the door. Suvi reached out for Kirsti in a quick, desperate way and then pulled Lucy to her too. There were tears running down her cheeks. Dad sagged with relief when he saw they were all right.

'Come in,' Mum said.

'I can wait in the car,' Suvi said, looking at my dad.

'No, Suvi. If you don't mind, I'd like it if you both came in,' Mum said. 'I think we need to talk to Lucy. All of us.'

So we all sat down in the sitting room, eight of us including Kirsti. Lucy gazed round at everyone. It was what she'd always wanted: all of us together in the same house. She looked miserable.

Dad sat down slowly and sucked in air through his nose. He looked exhausted. He took hold of Lucy's hand. 'I know you didn't mean Kirsti any harm, but you put both of you in danger.'

Lucy blinked.

'Promise me that you will never, ever take Kirsti anywhere, not even out to the garden, unless you have an adult with you.'

She'd already promised Mum and usually Lucy is always pointing out what she has already done and complaining if someone expects her to do the same thing twice, but she just bowed her head and said, 'I promise.'

'You've frightened us all horribly. We had to call the police. You could have been hurt.'

Lucy's face was tight with shame and misery. 'I didn't mean to! It wasn't meant to be scary for you.'

'I just don't understand why you'd do such a silly thing.'

Lucy was gulping.

'She's been missing Kirsti,' Mum said.

'I know,' Dad said. 'And we've always been

quite happy for her to come round and say hello. She's very wel—'

'Lucy was hoping that we could all live together,' Mum said.

Dad stopped talking.

'In fact, she's cleaned and redecorated the basement, in the hope that you three could move in down there.'

Mum looked at Dad, Dad looked at Suvi, Suvi looked at Mum. All the adults in the room were having some sort of conversation with their eyes.

'It's really nice!' Lucy said hopefully. 'I did it properly!'

Mum looked like she might cry.

Dad pulled Lucy on to his lap. 'I'm very sorry, sweetheart, but we can't live here.'

'Why not?'

'Because we've got our own home. And that's your home as well; you've got two houses now because you belong to two families. And I know that can be a bit complicated and I know your homes are a bit different, but I want you to try to enjoy both of them.'

His forehead scrunched in the effort of trying to get things to make sense to Lucy, but I don't think their divorce will ever really make sense to us.

'Some people don't mix,' Dad said. 'You don't

mush up your chips with your ice cream, do you? You enjoy those things separately. Try and think about your life as if it's a lovely meal with different courses.'

'I don't want that!' Tears were streaming down Lucy's face. 'I don't want a meal! I want everybody all mixed in together. Like a pie! In one big pie!'

Everybody in the room had wet eyes by now. 'I know you do,' Dad said. 'And I'm really sorry, Lucy, but you can't have it.'

And Mum, Dad and Suvi all said a lot more things after that, but basically they all meant just the same thing: no matter how much you wish things were different, you can't always have what you want.

CHAPTER ❤ THIRTY-TWO

Sometimes there isn't a happy ending to difficult stuff that happens in your life. But sometimes, if you have a lot of people to help you with it, you can start to learn to live with it.

There wasn't any magic solution to our family living in two different places; Lucy was always going to find that hard. And, even though we were older, me, Chloe and Amelia were going to find it hard too. But over the next few days Mum, Dad and Suvi all helped us feel a bit better about it.

They explained that it's a good thing that our family cares so much about each other and they helped Lucy think of ways to cope with feeling sad. Lucy is going to read Kirsti a goodnight story every night. If she's not at Dad's house, she'll do it by Skype.

Because it was half-term, we went to Dad's house on Wednesday for the whole day. Lucy was still subdued, but I started to think that it was true what Mum said about arguments letting people know how you feel because it does seem like the upset and shouting in the last couple of months have helped us all understand each other a bit better. When Mum dropped us off, she came into Dad's house and had a cup of tea. She held Kirsti and she talked to Dad and Suvi. It felt like maybe the two halves of our family aren't so horribly far apart. I don't think my mum is ever exactly going to be super good friends with Dad and Suvi, but it's nice to feel that they don't hate each other and can all talk together about important stuff.

After Mum had gone, Chloe said, 'What's the Plan?'

And Dad said he thought we should all make the Plans together from now on. We chose to play Cluedo and Dad didn't switch on the football or check his phone once. But he did ask me what I thought when Amelia and Chloe were having quite a loud discussion about whether belly rings are ridiculous.

On Thursday, the day of my sleepover, Lucy had cheered up enough to help me make a cushion mountain in the Pit and to lick the bowl that Chloe made the brownies in. Amelia and me blew up balloons and strung up the flower garlands.

'Do you remember at the beginning of term when you said I was nice?' I asked Amelia.

'Yep. You are.'

Lucy and Chloe came in with plates of food to put on the table.

'Isn't Ella nice?' Amelia asked them.

'Definitely,' Chloe said.

Lucy nodded.

'But what does that mean? Doesn't it mean a bit . . . not anything much?'

'No way!' Amelia said. 'It's hard work being nice. I should know. I've been trying it for the last week and I can only really manage it some of the time.'

'Nice means lots of things,' Chloe said. 'It's about thinking about other people's feelings. I didn't know that that was important, but you always do it.'

'Do I?'

'Yep,' Lucy said. 'You helped me get the paint and you wouldn't let Amelia in the Pit when I didn't want anyone in here.'

'And you were nice to Suvi,' Amelia said. 'We didn't even realise she needed being nice to.'

Amelia hadn't called Suvi the Ice Queen once since she saw her crying over Lucy and Kirsti.

'And me,' Chloe said. 'You knew that I couldn't understand Thunder and Amelia and all their feelings stuff, and you helped me work it out.'

'And you've been nice to Alenka in your class by asking her to join Hockey Club and including her in other things,' Amelia said. 'Her sister told me.'

Chloe nodded. 'And then there's Ash and Kay. And Mum.'

'You're the nicest person I know,' Amelia said, 'and that's a really, really good thing.'

Even though Amelia has been trying not to be mean lately, she still doesn't say stuff just to make people feel better so I believed her.

Ash, Kay, Erica, Alenka and also Jess and Nisha from Hockey Club all arrived on time. I thought that was probably everyone, but then the bell rang again and there were Jasmine's friends, Asia and Courtney.

They looked a bit sheepish. 'Jasmine didn't want us to come,' Asia said.

'But we thought it was really nice of you to invite us,' Courtney said and she gave me a box of cupcakes, fancy ones with swirly icing and tiny little gold stars on.

We put on some music and everyone spread out on the cushions, eating brownies and cupcakes and chatting.

I looked at Kayleigh drawing a cartoon of Chloe with cake icing on her nose. Ashandra was sitting next to her, reading the back of one of Amelia's books.

I know they are different.

'That's good,' Ashandra said, looking up and tapping Kayleigh's drawing.

But I know that we can all get on.

Chloe and Thunder were having a competition to see how many Jaffa cakes they could fit in their mouths.

Amelia was making Courtney and Asia crack up by saying something that probably wasn't very polite and Lucy was sitting on the table, wearing a crown she'd made out of the leftover tissue paper.

I love my sisters. They are loud and funny and brimming with self-confidence. But I don't have to be exactly like them. All these people came to my party and I don't have to put on an act or pretend to be someone else: they came to see me. I am a nice person. And that means something good. I don't want to be anybody else. Like my dad said, I'm perfectly Ella and that's not a bad thing to be at all.

Can't get enough of the
STRAWBERRY SISTERS?

Want to know how to throw your own
Whoopee? How to bake Chloe's special
cupcakes? Or which STRAWBERRY SISTER
you're most like?

Then turn the page for some fun extras!

STRAWBERRY SISTERS PROFILES

AMELIA
Age: 13

🍓 Hobbies: singing about sad things, painting her nails black and being sarcastic

🍓 Favourite food: pizza

🍓 Favourite phrase: 'That's a stupid idea'

🍓 Dream job: singer in a band

CHLOE
Age: 12

🍓 Hobbies: wrestling, hockey, rugby (if you can knock your teeth out doing it, Chloe loves it)

🍓 Favourite food: curry, chocolate and cake (sometimes all at the same time)

🍓 Favourite phrase: 'Can I have some more?'

🍓 Dream job: crisp taster

ELLA
Age: 11

🍓 Hobbies: making films with Ashandra and karaoke with Kayleigh

🍓 Favourite food: brownies

🍓 Favourite phrase: **'I'll do it'**

🍓 Dream job: working with numbers and nice people

LUCY
Age: 7

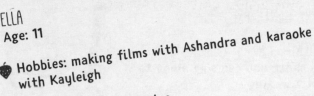

🍓 Hobbies: ballet, magic and being a bat

🍓 Favourite food: spaghetti with tomato ketchup

🍓 Favourite phrase: **'NO!'**

🍓 Dream job: magician or Bat Queen

KIRSTI
Age: 0

🍓 Hobbies: dribbling, sleeping and gurgling

🍓 Favourite food: milk

🍓 Favourtie phrase: **'Waaaaaaaaah!'**

🍓 Dream job: cot tester

WHICH STRAWBERRY SISTER ARE YOU?

WHAT'S YOUR FAVOURITE KIND OF MUSIC?
a) Cheerful pop music you can sing along to
b) Something with wailing
c) Anything LOUD
d) You prefer to make your own music

MUM SAYS IT'S TIME TO TIDY YOUR ROOM, WHAT'S YOUR RESPONSE?
a) Sort out your books alphabetically and your socks by colour.
Then maybe give your sister a hand with her half of the bedroom.
b) Sulking
c) You make it fun by seeing if you can throw or kick everything
into the right place
d) You build a cardboard prison and tidy all your toys into that

WHAT WOULD YOU RATHER WATCH ON TV?
a) A good film with a happy ending
b) A good film with a miserable ending
c) A football match
d) A magic show where someone gets chained up underwater

WHAT'S YOUR FAVOURITE COLOUR?
a) Purple
b) Black
c) Neon green
d) All of them

HOW MANY FRIENDS HAVE YOU GOT?
a) One or two really good ones
b) You're in a gang of six or eight
c) Too many to count
d) Lots, but they're always changing because you get rid of the
ones that you're bored with

HOW DO YOU LIKE TO SPEND THE WEEKEND?
a) Hanging out with your friends and family and doing your homework
b) In your room. Listening to music. Alone.
c) Swimming, shouting and eating
d) Working on secret projects

WHAT'S YOUR BEST SUBJECT AT SCHOOL?
a) Maths
b) Music
c) PE
d) Making the teacher cry

WHAT'S YOUR FAVOURITE ANIMAL?
a) Rabbits
b) Cats
c) Dogs, especially ones that can do tricks
d) Bats or anything with really sharp teeth

WHAT ARE YOU GOOD AT?
a) Being kind to people
b) Performing
c) Sport and eating
d) Everything

WHERE WOULD YOU GO ON YOUR DREAM HOLIDAY?
a) The seaside
b) A teens-only holiday camp
c) A caravan park with a swimming pool and lots of entertainment
d) The jungle

WHAT'S YOUR FAVOURITE OUTFIT?
a) Jeans and a comfy top
b) Black jeans, black shirt, black hat
c) A t-shirt with a monkey on and a hat with a straw and a place to put your drink
d) Snow boots and a tutu

MOSTLY 'A'S

You're like Ella. You like doing well at school and having fun. You don't like being the centre of attention. You're kind and thoughtful and an excellent friend.

MOSTLY 'B'S

You're like Amelia. You're a natural leader and you enjoy being centre stage. You hate tidying up and people messing with your stuff. You've got lots of friends who think you're funny and smart.

MOSTLY 'C'S

You're like Chloe. You love sport, food and playing practical jokes. Your favourite way to spend the day is hanging out with all your friends having really noisy fun.

MOSTLY 'D'S

You're like Lucy. You don't like school or being neat, and you hate being told what to do. Grown-ups sometimes think you're a bit rude, but because you're so lively and inventive you always have plenty of friends.

ELLA'S EXCELLENT GUIDE TO HAVING A WHOOPEE

1. Wait for someone in your family or one of your friends to do well at something. It can be anything really; top marks in a test, learning to swim, passing a music exam. Once we had a Whoopee because Lucy had managed not to be told off at school for a whole week.

2. Choose a present. Whoopee presents are always homemade. You might want to make a bracelet like Chloe or you could knit a scarf, paint a picture or even write a special letter like Amelia.

3. Decorate the bedroom of the person who has done well. Sometimes we use tinsel, but you could make paper chains or use balloons. See Amelia's instructions for how to make tissue paper flowers like we did.

4. Prepare refreshments. Juice and biscuits are fine. Or you if you have time could use Chloe's recipe for cupcakes.

5. Time to party! Music is a good idea to get people in the right mood. We like playing games (charades and March of the Zombies) and we always chat about the reason we're celebrating because that makes the Whoopee person feel really special.

6. Don't forget to say 'Whoopee!' a lot.

7. Everybody in my family always helps to tidy up after a Whoopee (even Lucy) because that way we know that Mum won't mind the next time we want to have one.

AMELIA'S QUITE BOSSY INSTRUCTIONS FOR MAKING TISSUE PAPER FLOWERS

1. Take four sheets of tissue paper and place them on top of each other (You can use more sheets if you want a fluffier flower but we haven't got many pieces left in our house because Lucy used it all up making tutus for her dinosaurs).

2. Fold in half (short edge to short edge).

3. Starting at one of the short edges, fold the stack of paper over about 5cm, then turn the paper over and fold back in the opposite direction. Keep folding back and forth (Chloe says this is like making a fan) until all the paper is folded.

4. Tie the 'fan' in the middle with a piece of cotton or string, as tight as you can.

5. At either end of the 'fan' cut a rounded shape like the end of a petal, or you can cut it into a point like Lucy did because she likes spikey stuff.

6. Open out the 'fan' then (this is the cool part) gently separate all the layers of tissue and fluff them into a ball-ish shape

7. You can dangle single flowers from the ceiling by a thread or you can string a lot together with a ribbon to make a garland. Make sure you tie the thread or ribbon around the middle part of the flower, don't use the petals – they'll tear easily.

CHLOE'S RECIPE FOR WHOOPEE CUPCAKES

INGREDIENTS
125G SELF-RAISING FLOUR
125G BUTTER
125G CASTER SUGAR
2 EGGS
FOR THE ICING
150G ICING SUGAR
2 TABLESPOONS OF WARM WATER

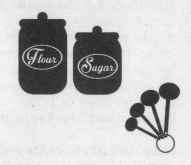

YOU'LL ALSO NEED ABOUT 24 PAPER CAKE CASES

Ask an adult to preheat the oven to 180 or gas mark 4. If your big sister offers to do it, you can annoy her by saying, 'You're not a grown up'.

Cream the butter and the sugar in a mixing bowl (this just means smooshing them with a wooden spoon until the sugar is all mixed in).

Add the eggs one by one and stir some more (WARNING: it's safer to crack your eggs on the side of the bowl than on your head, I tried that once and, let me tell you, egg doesn't make very good shampoo).

Sieve the flour into the bowl and stir again.

Put your cake cases into a twelve hole bun tray. We've only got one bun tray so that means we have to cook them in two goes because twelve cakes doesn't go very far in my family.

Use a teaspoon to dollop the mixture into the cases. Mum says the best way to do this is to use your little finger to slide the

mixture off the spoon and into the
case, that way you only get one sticky finger.
I say, the more sticky fingers you get, the more licky
fingers you get.

Get your adult to put the cakes in the oven. They should be done
in 10-12 minutes. You can tell that they're finished when the tops
go golden brown or, if you live in my house, when Lucy says, 'Are
they ready yet?' for the millionth time.

Leave the cakes to cool for as long as you can bear. An hour is
good.

Sieve the icing sugar into a small bowl. I always pretend I'm the
witch of winter making it snow when I do this.

Add the water and stir. You want the icing to be quite thick, if
it's too runny it will slide right off the cakes. If it's really stiff
add a few more drops of water, if it's too wet sprinkle in a bit
more icing sugar, but be careful - once, I kept on adding more
water then more icing sugar and I ended up with pints and pints
of icing (I thought it was nice on cereal but no one else agreed).

Dribble the icing on the cakes with a teaspoon - you can use the
back of the spoon to smooth it out.

While the icing is still wet add any kind of decoration you like
- sprinkles, chocolate drops, tiny sweets. I like all three together,
but Lucy prefers plastic spiders.

Do the washing up, or pay Ella with cakes to do it for you.

Just like Ella, Candy Harper grew up in a rather small house with a rather large family. As the fourth of five sisters it was often hard to get a word in edgeways, so she started writing down her best ideas. It's probably not a coincidence that her first 'book' featured an orphan living in deserted castle.

Growing up, she attended six different schools, but that honestly had very little to do with an early interest in explosives.

Candy has been a bookseller, a teacher and the person who puts those little stickers on apples. She is married and has a daughter named after Philip Pullman's Lyra.

You can follow her on Twitter @CandyHarper_